The Little Big Book for
GRANDMOTHERS

Edited by LENA TABORI and ALICE WONG
Designed by TIMOTHY SHANER

welcome
BOOKS
NEW YORK · SAN FRANCISCO

Published in 2002 by Welcome Books
An imprint of Welcome Enterprises, Inc.
6 West 18th Street, 3rd Floor, New York, NY 10011
(212) 989-3200; Fax (212) 989-3205
email: info@welcomebooks.biz
www.welcomebooks.biz

Project Director: Alice Wong
Project Assistants: Lawrence Chesler and Nicholas Liu
Fairy Tales retold by Sara Baysinger
Activities by Jacinta O'Halloran and Alice Wong
Musical arrangement by Frank Zuback
Finger games illustrations by Megan Halsey
Illustrations on page 53 by Lawrence Chesler
Recipes by Natasha Tabori Fried and Lena Tabori
Selected art courtesy of Ingrid Innes

Front jacket illustration by Jessie Willcox Smith

Distributed to the trade in the U.S. and Canada by
Andrews McMeel Distribution Services
Order Department and Customer Service (800) 223-2336
Orders Only Fax: (800) 943-9831

Library of Congress Control Number: 2001056810

Printed in Singapore
First Edition
10 9 8 7 6 5 4 3 2

To - Grandma   May 2003
From, Robbie, Tina & Rob

DEDICATION

Over the river
and through
the woods to
Grandmother's
house we go...

Contents

Contents

Contents

Contents

Dearer than our children are
the children of our children.

—Egyptian proverb

Foreword

I remember standing on a little stool while my grandmother sewed gold jewelry to the inside of my dress. I was almost five years old and I was going to America with my parents and little brother. It was more than eight years before I saw my grandmother again. My grandfather passed away; she came to live with us and we shared a bedroom for the next eight years. Every morning, she combed her silvery gray hair into a bun, pinning it at the nape of her neck with several bobby pins. She always wore Chinese silk suits with high mandarin collars and intricately sewn fabric buttons. She sat with both legs crossed and tucked under her, even at the dinner table. She liked to rock back and forth gently while she talked, and she covered her mouth when she laughed. We stayed up late at night and she talked softly of her life, of siblings and children she lost during the war, of my mother's childhood, of Chinese ways and superstitions. When I started to come home late, I had both my mother and my grandmother waiting up for me.

I wept so at her memorial service, but it was one of my

Foreword

life's most defining moments. While I cried I realized that it was okay. It was okay, because I looked around me and saw my grandmother's seven children and fifteen grandchildren. From her came so many lives. I was the eldest grandchild and the youngest was just two years old. He was running around with another young cousin, both happy in their toddler world. I picked him up and was comforted.

I have two little ones of my own now: Eve, six, and Sylvia, four. They are blessed with two wonderful grandmothers: my mom, Pau Pau (Chinese for maternal grandmother), and my mother-in-law, Dids (a nickname from her childhood). Pau Pau takes care of them while I work; she has done this since their birth. At Pau Pau's, there are a different set of rules—they get away with (and get) stuff I would never allow. I'm always glad for the reprieve the girls get from my discipline.

Almost every weekend, we drive to Pennsylvania, where my in-laws have a barn in the country—complete with chickens. The girls gather eggs, pick tomatoes, rake leaves, bake cookies, catch fireflies and caterpillars and crickets, fly kites, watch for deer and wild turkey, and go sledding in the snow. They sing and dance to Roy Orbison and watch Charlie Chaplin and Fred

Foreword

Astaire. Holidays are especially wonderful. Dids gives us Easter-egg hunts, July 4th sparklers, nine-foot Christmas trees, and spectacular Thanksgiving and Christmas dinners beside a blazing fireplace. Eve and Sylvia are bright, happy, and confident girls because they are surrounded by a loving family.

I dedicate this book to the three grandmothers in my life—for all my memories and the wonderful memories my daughters are forming.

When we published *The Little Big Book for Moms* in May 2000, we received calls and letters from grandmothers all over the country. They were buying multiple copies of the book for their daughters and daughters-in-law. One grandmother described how she copies the illustrations from the book to embroider on pillows for her grandchildren. Another talked about how wonderful it was to find her old favorites in the book to read to her grandchildren. It is time for grandmothers to have a *Little Big Book* of their own. Here it is, created with care and with visions of happy children, loved and indulged. Read, cook, bake, sing, play, do, and have fun! May your little ones treasure their memories with you always.

—Alice Wong

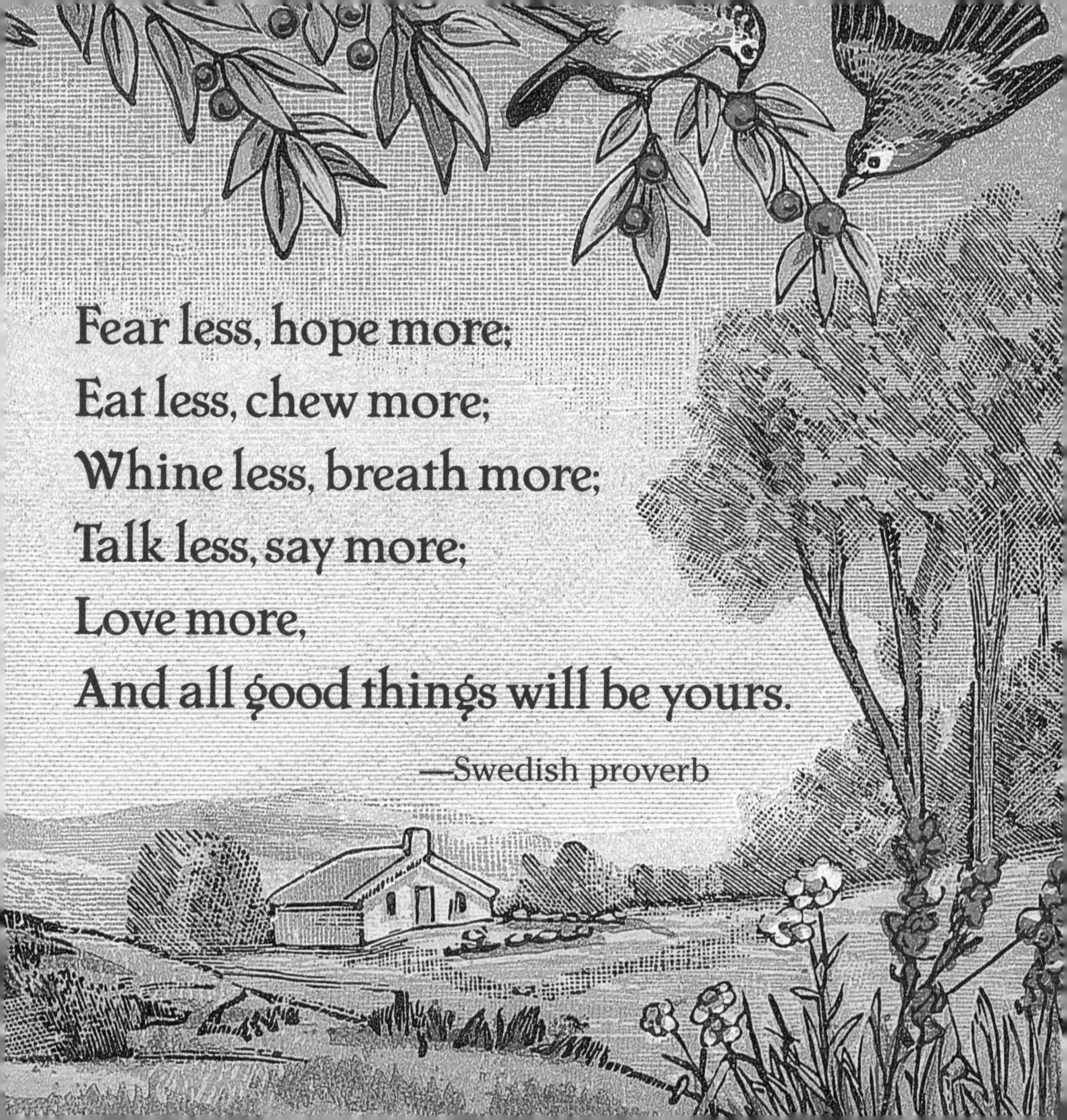

Fear less, hope more;

Eat less, chew more;

Whine less, breath more;

Talk less, say more;

Love more,

And all good things will be yours.

—Swedish proverb

The Old Woman
Who Was Right

nce upon a time there was an old couple who fought all the time. The husband complained that he did all the work — chopping wood, hunting game, and making repairs — while the wife argued that she was plenty busy cooking, cleaning, and mending his clothes. Well, the wife got fed up with her husband's crabbing, so she offered him a deal: "Tomorrow we'll switch jobs. You stay home and keep house, while I go do your work."

This suited her husband just fine. "Women's work is easy," he said. "But you're too weak to do my share."

"We'll see about that," the woman laughed. "We'll see whether I'm too weak, or if you're not bright enough to do my work."

So it was settled. The next morning the old woman rose early and headed off to the forest with her husband's axe and rifle in hand. The old man continued to snore, for he didn't imagine that

The Old Woman Who Was Right

women's work could take all day.

Around noon, he was awakened from his deep sleep by a knock at the door. His youngest daughter had come to drop off her baby, as she did each day on her way into town. The child was sleeping when its mother left, but before long it woke and screamed with hunger. The old man gave the baby a bottle of cow's milk, and this reminded him that he was supposed to put the cow out to pasture.

He didn't think he should leave the child alone for the time it would take him to lead the cow out to the grassy field. So he got the idea to bring the cow to the sod roof of their home, where tall grass had sprouted that spring. Pleased with himself for his cleverness, the old man found a plank and walked the cow up to the roof. And, just to be safe, he tied a long rope around the cow's middle, dropped the end of the rope down the chimney, and tied the other end to his own ankle once he got inside.

The old man decided that he'd better start dinner,

The Old Woman Who Was Right

so he put the pot on the stove to boil. Then he sat down to churn
the butter, but then thought that he should first bake the bread.
He put together the ingredients, as best as he knew how, and put
the dough in the oven to bake. But he hadn't added the yeast, so
the bread was sure to burn. The pot boiled, so he went over to stir
it. He lifted the lid, and was reminded that he hadn't yet put
anything in the stew. He picked up the baby and went out to the
garden, where he collected carrots, potatoes, an onion, and some
parsley. He returned to the pot and
threw everything in, as is!

    He played with the baby until
its mother came again. Then he went to
the cellar to quench his enormous thirst.
No sooner had he unplugged a barrel of
ale than he heard the pig grunting and
squealing in the kitchen. The old
man had forgotten to take the pig its
breakfast, so the pig had broken out of its
pen and was searching for food. By the
time the old man caught the pig, it had knocked over the butter
churn and made a complete mess with the cream. The old man tied
the pig out by the front door with some leftover scraps of food. He

came in to see smoke coming from the oven. Then he remembered that he had left the ale barrel unplugged, and he raced down the stairs to find all the ale had run out onto the cellar floor. As he was mopping up the mess, the cow fell from the roof, dragging the old man up the stairs and into the chimney. There he stuck; and the cow hung halfway between the roof and the ground, swinging from its middle on the long rope.

When the old woman returned home, she got quite a scare. Smoke was pouring out of the house, the cow was hanging from the roof, and her husband was nowhere in sight. She ran to the cow and cut it down from the rope. She raced inside to find her husband in a heap by the fireplace. He was bumped and bruised and half suffocated.

She had returned with stacks of firewood, and two fat geese. But she did not rub this in her poor husband's face. Instead, she led him to the bed, and took the burned bread from the oven and the pot from the stove. She tended to his bumps and bruises and kissed him on the forehead. As she got up to leave him resting, he said, "You were right to change places with me, old woman. Now I see that it is not easy to be in your shoes." Then he fell asleep.

After that day, the old man no longer complained or crabbed. He had only praise and admiration for his hardworking wife. ✦

19

Grandma's Glasses

Here are Grandma's glasses,	And here is Grandma's hat,	This is the way she folds her hands and lays them in her lap.

Here are Grandpa's glasses,	Here is Grandpa's hat,	This is the way he folds his arms, Just like that.

The Sweetie Shop

by Jessie Pope

There are all sorts of shops
   In our little town:
One sells us nice cakes,
   Kept by old Mrs. Brown;
One sells us new frocks,
   When for Sunday we're dressed—
But the shop that sells sweeties
   We all like the best!

That's the shop where we go
   When we each have a penny,
But we stand round the window
   If we haven't any.

There are sweets in the bottles,
   And more on the shelves,
And we each choose the kind
   We like best for ourselves.

I'm fondest of toffees,
   But Jack prefers choc,
And Joan loves those sticks
   Of bright-colored rock.
We rush there with pennies
   Before it's too late,
And the shopkeeper gives us
   Extremely good weight!

The Big Rock Candy Mountain

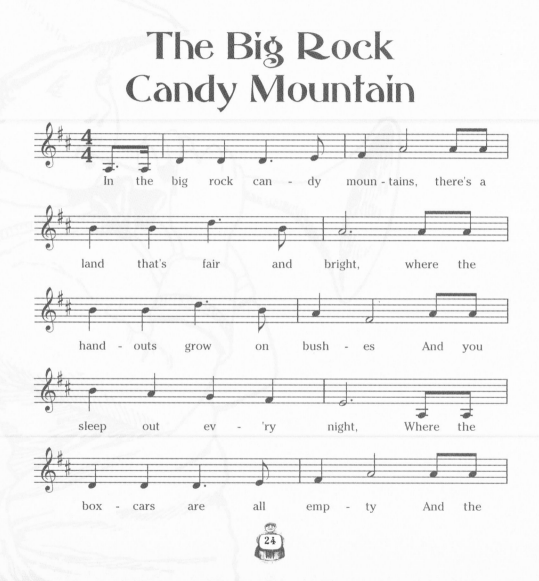

In the big rock can - dy moun - tains, there's a land that's fair and bright, where the hand - outs grow on bush - es And you sleep out ev - 'ry night, Where the box - cars are all emp - ty And the

The Big Rock Candy Mountain

sun shines ev - 'ry day, Oh, I'm

bound to go where there ain't no snow, Where the

rain don't fall and the wind don't blow, In the

big rock can - dy moun - tains.

Chorus

Oh, the buz - zin' of the bees in the

The Big Rock Candy Mountain

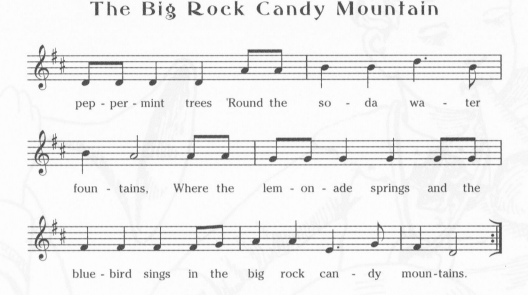

pep - per - mint trees 'Round the so - da wa - ter

foun - tains, Where the lem - on - ade springs and the

blue - bird sings in the big rock can - dy moun - tains.

2. In the Big Rock Candy Mountains,
   You never change your socks,
   And little streams of lemonade
   Come a-tricklin' down the rocks,
   The hobos there are friendly
   And their fires all burn bright,
   There's a lake of stew and soda, too,
   You can paddle all around 'em in a big canoe
   In the Big Rock Candy Mountains.

   Chorus

Lemon Squares

The next time you serve up a snack for your grandchildren, try some of these zesty lemon tarts. With a perfectly textured crust and creamy filling, they are fabulous!

CRUST

3 1/2 cups all-purpose white flour
1/4 cup confectioners' sugar
1/4 teaspoon salt
28 tablespoons (3 1/2 sticks) unsalted butter, cut into bits

1. Preheat the oven to 350°F.

2. In a large bowl, sift together the flour, sugar, and salt. With a pastry blender or two knives, cut the butter into the flour mixture until it has the consistency of cornmeal.

3. Press the dough onto a large baking sheet (10" x 15", with 2-inch-high sides).

4. Bake for 20 minutes.

FILLING

6 large eggs
3 cups granulated sugar
2 tablespoons grated lemon zest
3/4 cup lemon juice
2/3 cup all-purpose white flour
1 teaspoon baking powder
Confectioners' sugar for dusting

1. While the crust is baking, beat the eggs until blended and then beat in the following ingredients slowly, in this order: sugar, lemon zest, lemon juice, flour and baking powder. Blend until smooth.

2. Pour the mixture over the crust and bake for 25 more minutes.

3. Cool in the pan set up on a rack. Using a sharp knife, carefully cut into squares and dust with confectioners' sugar.

Makes about thirty-six 2-inch squares.

Chocolate Fudge

Chocolate fudge is the stuff of sweet dreams! Imagine your grandchildren with a light dusting of sugar on their faces and syrup dripping off their fingers on a lazy Sunday afternoon. The smell of chocolate and the sound of laughter fill the air. All wait impatiently for the fudge to cool—and then, a taste of heaven.

1 cup sugar
1 cup cocoa powder
6 teaspoons butter
1/4 cup milk
1 tablespoon light corn syrup
1 tablespoon vanilla extract
3 cups confectioners' sugar, sifted
1 cup chopped nuts (optional)

1. In a medium-size saucepan combine sugar, cocoa powder, butter, milk, and corn syrup. Mix well and bring to a low boil. Allow mixture to boil for three minutes, stirring constantly.

2. Turn heat down to low and, stirring constantly, add vanilla and confectioners' sugar. Stir until completely smooth. Add nuts if desired.

3. Turn mixture onto a buttered 8" x 8" square buttered pan and pat out. Once mixture has cooled, cut into 1-inch squares. Fudge can be stored at room temperature in an airtight container for three or four days.

Makes sixty-four 1-inch squares.

Valentine's Day

Celebrate Valentine's Day with flowers and hearts. Let your grandchildren declare their love to their favorite people with these two simple activities. Tissue paper flowers last so much longer than real flowers! Write multiple messages of love on the chain of love or hang it as decoration to show how much love is in the air.

TISSUE PAPER FLOWER

Tissue paper (red, pink, yellow), green pipe cleaners, perfume (optional)

1. Lay 3 or 4 sheets of tissue paper on top of each other.

2. Working with the shorter side, fold the tissue paper back and forth as if making a paper fan. Continue until you have folded the entire length.

3. Wrap a pipe cleaner tightly around the middle of the folded paper.

4. Separate the tissue paper by lifting each piece and pulling it toward the center to "fluff out" the petals of the flower.

5. Spray a bit of perfume into the air several inches above the flower.

CHAINS OF LOVE

Red or pink crepe-paper streamers, marker, scissors, tape

1. Fold a square at one end of streamer. Continue folding accordion style until you have a stack of squares.

2. Draw a heart on the top square: Make sure the sides of the heart "overflow" the side edges of the square so the hearts will remain connected after cutting.

3. Cut out the top and bottom of the heart shape, leaving at least $1/2$ inch connected at the sides. (You may have to divide the streamer into sections for easier cutting through multiple layers. You can tape back together.)

4. Unfold and hang your chain of hearts.

Variation: To make a valentine card, use a strip of construction paper. Write words of love on each heart and decorate with glitter.

Jorinda and Jorindel

nce upon a time there was a wicked witch who lived in an old castle in the middle of the forest. During the day, she flew through the forest in the form of a screech owl or crept about the castle grounds in the form of a cat. But at night, she changed herself back into an old woman. Whenever a young man came too near her castle, she would freeze him in his tracks, and he could not move until she set him free. And whenever a young woman came too close, the witch changed her into a bird and trapped her in a cage. She had captured seven hundred girls this way, and had seven hundred birds in the castle.

One afternoon, a beautiful girl named Jorinda went for a long walk in the forest with her sweetheart, Jorindel. When the last rays of the sun were shining through the trees, Jorinda and Jorindel decided it was time to turn back. But it was getting dark and they couldn't remember which way to go. Growing more and more frightened, they quickly walked in the direction they

Jorinda and Jorindel

thought would lead them home. Jorinda began to sing softly to calm herself. But her song stopped when the sweethearts arrived at the base of the hideous castle!

Jorindel shook with fear, because he had heard the stories of boys turned to stone and girls turned to caged birds. He turned to grab for Jorinda's hand, but she was gone. A nightingale was in her place, singing its sad song. Jorindel knew this must be his beloved Jorinda, turned into a bird. He began to weep, but his tears froze in his eyes. The witch's spell held him still.

Soon the old woman appeared and caught the nightingale in her cage. She quickly disappeared up the castle steps, and Jorindel found himself free again. He wanted to follow the witch into the castle, but decided it would be better to go away and make a plan for how to free his loved one.

Jorindel returned home and asked his family and friends what he should do, but no one had any good advice. Finally, one night he had a dream that he found a delicate purple flower that contained a rare pearl. He dreamed that he plucked the flower, took it to the old castle, and freed his dear Jorinda.

Jorinda and Jorindel

In the morning, he began to search the countryside for the purple flower, but after eight long days he still had not found it. Finally, on the ninth day, he found the flower. But instead of discovering a pearl inside its petals, Jorindel found a large dewdrop. He plucked the flower and set out for the castle.

He walked until dusk, and then spotted the castle just ahead. He approached the door and was glad to see that nothing happened to him. Jorindel touched the flower to the door, and it sprang open. He entered the castle and followed the sound of the birds singing.

At last he came to the chamber with the seven hundred birds singing in the seven hundred cages. The witch appeared, but she could not approach Jorindel as long as he held the magical flower. Jorindel looked around at the birds and wondered how he would find his Jorinda. Luckily, he noticed the witch trying to escape with one of the cages. He caught the witch by the arm and touched the cage with the flower; and the beautiful Jorinda appeared before him. Then Jorindel touched all the cages with the special flower so that the birds turned back into hundreds of maidens. Jorinda threw her arms around Jorindel's neck and cried tears of joy. The two returned home and lived happily ever after. ✦

Fox and Hen

One of the players is chosen to be the fox and another to be the hen. All the others are chicks. They form a line behind the hen, one behind another, each holding on to the waist of the child in front. The hen spreads her arms wide to protect her chicks while the fox, in front of her, tries to run past her arms to grab a chick from the line. The game is over when all the chicks are captured.

Freeze Tag

Children scatter in an open area before one player, who is "It," chases after them. Whoever "It" tags must freeze like ice on the spot until an unfrozen player is able to tag and unfreeze them. The child who is "It" must tag and freeze all the children, chasing new ones down as well as guarding already frozen victims. To make the game easier, players can remain frozen, and not be "melted" or saved.

HIDE-AND-SEEK

One child dubbed "It" hides his or her eyes at a spot called "home" and counts to twenty. The other children run away and hide. The child who is "It" calls out "Ready or not, here I come!" and begins searching for the other players. He or she must catch a player before they scramble to safety at "home." The one caught is "It" next time. If none are caught, then the child who is "It" remains so for another round.

A-Tisket, A-Tasket

A - tis - ket, a - tas - ket, a green and yel-low bas - ket. I
wrote a let - ter to my love and on the way I dropped it. I
dropped it, I dropped it, and on the way I dropped it. A
lit - tle boy picked it up and put it in his pock - et.

39

Curly-Locks

Curly-Locks, Curly-Locks,
wilt thou be mine?

Thou shalt not wash the dishes,
nor yet feed the swine;

But sit on a cushion,
and sew a fine seam,

And feed upon strawberries,
sugar, and cream.

41

Blueberry Corn Muffins

Breakfast at Grandmother's house is special. Gently wake up your grandchildren with the aroma of baking muffins. What a wonderful way to greet the morning! Serve these warm with homemade jams *(page 271)*, sit back, and enjoy the sight of your little ones' blueberry- and jam-smeared faces.

$1^1/_2$ cups yellow cornmeal
$1^1/_2$ cups sifted white flour
$3/_4$ cup white sugar
$4^1/_2$ teaspoons baking powder
1 teaspoon salt
3 teaspoons butter, softened
3 eggs
$1^1/_2$ cups milk
1 cup blueberries

1. Preheat the oven to 425°F.

2. In a large bowl, combine dry ingredients and cut in butter.

3. In a separate bowl, beat together the eggs and then beat in the milk. Add to the dry ingredients and mix well.

4. Stir in blueberries.

5. Spoon batter into greased muffin pans. Bake 15 to 20 minutes, until tops are golden brown and an inserted fork comes out clean.

Makes twelve to sixteen large muffins.

Grandmother Says...

Early to bed and early to rise, make a man healthy, wealthy, and wise.

If a job's worth doing, it's worth doing well.

There is a time and a place for everything.

Two heads are better than one.

Necessity is the mother of invention.

44

A rolling stone gathers
no moss.

*T*ime and tide wait
for no man.

*T*ime cures all things.

*T*omorrow is another day.

*M*any hands make light work.

*T*here's no place like home.

An apple a day keeps the doctor away.

Grandmother's Valentine

"Secrets, Fido! You must not tell." Jean shook a finger in her little dog's face. "You must not tell anyone," she added.

Fido didn't know what secrets were, but he did know that when Jean held up her finger it meant that there was something to be careful about; so he wagged his bit of tail and smothered a bark.

"I'll tell you about it," said Jean, working away busily. "I've made one for Mother, one for Father, one for Jack, one for Susan, and I've six more almost finished. No one but you will see them until St. Valentine's Day, Fido."

Jean counted them again, one by one. "I haven't made one for Grandmother yet," she said thoughtfully. "Her valentine must be

Grandmother's Valentine

the best of them all, Fido, the loveliest and *best.*" She looked again at her valentines. They were of all sorts and sizes and colors—blue, pink, red, and gold. On some she had painted cupids with gauzy wings; others were covered with hearts pierced with tiny darts. One was wreathed with flowers as bright as those that grew in Grandmother's garden.

"They're beautiful," said Jean again, "but not one of them is what I wish for Grandmother. Hers must be different from the others."

Jean had been working all day, painting, cutting, and pasting. It had been easy to make a valentine for the members of her own family and for each one of her little friends; but it was hard to think of one which would carry her message of love to Grandmother. She placed all that she had made in a long row and looked thoughtfully at each one; but she was not satisfied. For some time she sat thinking. Fido wagged his tail and wondered what was the matter.

Grandmother's Valentine

Suddenly, she jumped to her feet and cried out, "I know what I'll do. But— O Fido, this time I shall not tell even you my secret!"

Fido wagged his tail and watched his little mistress gather up all the hearts, cupids, and paper lace she had left and put them together. Then she ran upstairs as fast as she could, calling to her little dog, who was close at her heels, "Not this time, Fido. You must not come with me this time."

In a moment Jean came down the stairs with something white in her arms. She ran into the next room where she had been making valentines and she locked the door.

As soon as supper was over Jean slipped out of the house and ran to the homes of her little friends in the neighborhood.

Under each door she slipped a valentine. But, strange to say, she did not leave one under Grandmother's door, although Grandmother lived but two houses away.

Grandmother's Valentine

Next morning when Jean's father went to the door he called out, "Come, come! See what St. Valentine has left for us." There, on the step, lay two beautiful valentines. Jean's mother came running to see the surprise. "There is no name on them," she said. "See the beautiful red hearts and dear little cupids."

Then Fido could keep still no longer. He wagged his stumpy tail as hard as he could and at the same time he leaped and barked with joy.

"Ha! ha!" laughed Mother. "Fido knows St. Valentine has been here. I must run over to Grandmother's and see if she, too, has had a visit from him."

Jean did not say a word, but as soon as her mother had left, the little girl ran to her room, changed her dress, and threw a big cloak about her. Then she and Fido ran as fast as they could to Grandmother's house, laughing all the way.

Grandmother's Valentine

She knocked at the door, threw off her cloak, and waited. She heard Grandmother's voice saying: "That sounds like my little girl's knock. I'm having several visitors this morning."

Grandmother opened the door. There stood Jean in a white dress all covered with red hearts and little cupids with flaming darts. Fido was dancing and barking around her.

In a minute Grandmother knew what it all meant. She threw her arms around her little girl and said:

"This is my valentine,
This is my dove;
This is the child
I dearly love."

Jell-O on the Plate

Jell-O on the plate,
Jell-O on the plate,
Wibble, wobble,
Wibble, wobble,
Jell-O on the plate.

(Rock baby from side to side)

Candies in the jar,
Candies in the jar,
Shake them up,
Shake them up,
Candies in the jar.

(Bounce baby up and down gently)

Candles on the cake,
Candles on the cake,
Blow them out,
Blow them out,
PUFF, PUFF, PUFF!

(Blow on baby)

53

Strawberry Shortcake

"**S**trawberry shortcake cream on top, tell me the name of your sweetheart." Grandmother is surely a sweetheart when she serves this classic favorite. Make the cakes ahead of time and let your grandchildren help assemble this pretty confection when they arrive.

3 cups sugar
16 tablespoons (2 sticks) butter,
   room temperature
6 eggs
8 ounces sour cream
2 tablespoons vanilla
4 cups flour
1/2 teaspoon baking soda
3 cups fresh whipped cream *(see page 81)*
2 pints fresh strawberries

1. Preheat oven to 350°F. Butter and flour two 8- or 9-inch layer pans. Set aside.

2. In a large bowl, cream together sugar and butter. Beat in eggs one at a time, then add sour cream and vanilla and mix well.

3. In a separate bowl, combine flour and baking soda, then add gradually to egg mixture.

4. Pour into prepared pans. Bake for 1 hour to an hour and 15 minutes. Let cool 30 minutes before turning cakes out of pans. Set aside and allow to cool completely.

5. While cakes are cooling, prepare whipped cream and refrigerate.

6. Rinse, clean, and halve strawberries. Set aside on paper towel.

7. Once cakes are cool, begin assembly. Slice each cake in half crosswise so that your shortcake has a total of four layers. Spread whipped cream over one layer, top with strawberries and the next layer of cake and repeat to build your cake.

Note: Cakes may be prepared up to 24 hours ahead of time. Strawberries and whipped cream may be prepared several hours ahead of time. But cake should not be assembled until less than an hour before serving, to prevent sogginess.

Makes one 8- or 9-inch cake.

Chocolate Layer Cake

This dense, yummy cake, spread with rich chocolate icing, is perfect for birthday celebrations. One bite and everyone will know this is something Grandmother made from scratch with a lot of love. Your grandchildren will melt with delight.

CAKE

2 1/4 cups white flour, sifted
1 1/2 cups white sugar
3 teaspoon baking powder
1 teaspoon salt
8 tablespoons (1 stick) butter,
    room temperature
2/3 cup milk
1 tablespoon vanilla
1/3 cup milk
2 eggs

CHOCOLATE ICING

1 stick (8 tablespoons butter)
4 squares unsweetened bakers' chocolate
1 box confectioners' sugar
1 tablespoon vanilla
1/3 cup milk

1. Heat oven to 350°F. Butter and flour two 8- or 9-inch layer pans. Set aside.

2. In a large bowl, mix together flour, sugar, baking powder, and salt.

3. Continue to mix, slowly adding butter, 2/3 cup milk, and vanilla. Beat vigorously.

4. Add another 1/3 cup milk and eggs. Beat for 2 minutes, then pour into baking pans. Bake 30 to 35 minutes. Let cool before turning out of pans.

5. To make the icing, melt butter and chocolate together in small saucepan.

6. Pour mixture into large bowl, add remaining ingredients and beat until smooth.

7. When cakes are completely cool, ice cake with chocolate.

Makes one 8- or 9-inch cake.

You've got to do
your own growing,
no matter how tall
your grandfather was.

—Irish proverb

Thumbkin

nce upon a time there was a poor woodsman and his wife and seven sons. The youngest boy was seven, and yet he was no bigger than his father's thumb; so his parents named him Thumbkin. He was the cleverest of all the boys, but no one knew this because he rarely spoke—he mostly watched and listened.

When winter came, the family had stored very little food. One night, when the boys were all in bed, the woodsman spoke with his wife. "We have no food, and our boys will surely starve. Tomorrow we must take them into the forest and leave them."

His wife was horrified at the thought. "We can't do that to them. It's far too cruel."

"In the forest, they might be saved by a miracle," said the woodsman. "But here, we can't help them." His wife wept, but had to agree.

Thumbkin, who was not yet asleep, heard every word. He

Thumbkin

quickly jumped out of his slipper bed, and snuck outside. He gathered many shiny pebbles, and stuffed them into his pockets before returning to bed.

The next morning, the woodsman led his seven boys deep into the forest. The boys gathered twigs while their father chopped wood. Slowly, the woodsman moved farther and farther away from his children, until he couldn't see them any longer. He returned home sad and alone.

When the boys realized that their father was gone, they became very frightened. But clever Thumbkin had dropped the shiny pebbles all along the path into the forest. He led his brothers home along the pebble trail. But they didn't understand why their father had abandoned them, and so were afraid to enter the house.

What the boys didn't know was that the woodsman had had a visitor while they were gone. A man who owed him money had come to repay him, and his wife bought lots of food. As the woodsman and his wife sat down to eat their first meal in days, the wife began to weep. "I wish our boys were here. I'd give them a great meal."

Thumbkin

Well, the boys heard her and entered the house, shouting,
"Here we are, Mother!" She hugged and kissed them and sat them
down for a delicious supper. The family ate well together, that
night and for the next week. But when the cupboards were nearly
empty, the woodsman told his wife again that he would have to
take his boys deep into the forest. Again Thumbkin heard him,
and hopped up to gather more shiny pebbles, but the door was
locked and he could not get outside.

The next day, as the boys left the house, their mother gave
them some bread for lunch. Thumbkin left a trail of breadcrumbs
to lead them home. Their father led them deep into the
forest, and as they gathered twigs, he left them alone.
Thumbkin was not worried, for he had left the
breadcrumb trail. But when he searched for
the crumbs, he discovered that the birds had
eaten them all.

The wind began to howl, and the lost boys
shook in their boots. Night fell, and with it a
cold, cold rain. Thumbkin climbed a tree to see what he
could see. Off in the distance, he saw a light. He got
down from the tree and led his brothers to a well-lit house
near the edge of the forest. They knocked at the door, and

Thumbkin

a woman answered. Thumbkin said, "We beg your pardon. My brothers and I are very lost. May we stay with you until tomorrow morning?"

"You poor things," cried the woman. "I am sorry, but I cannot keep you. This is an ogre's house, and he will eat you alive!"

The boys trembled from fright and the cold. "What can we do?" said Thumbkin. "If you don't let us in, the wolves will eat us. I think we should take our chances."

"Come in, then," said the ogre's housekeeper, "and warm up." So the boys filed in and dried their wet clothes by the fire. Then there was a loud pounding at the door. It was the ogre!!! The housekeeper quickly hid the boys under her bed and went to open the door.

The ogre stormed in and headed straight for his dinner. He started to eat, but got distracted.

"I smell live meat," he thundered.

"It must be the goat that I skinned," offered the woman.

"I smell live meat," roared the ogre. "You can't fool me." The ogre stood up and went straight for the bed. He threw it aside and pulled the boys up. "Six fine boys will make a nice dessert!" The ogre said six, for he did not see Thumbkin, though he was in plain view, because he was so small.

Thumbkin

The boys fell to their knees and begged for mercy, but the ogre just licked his lips and smiled. He was just about to munch on the first boy when the woman said, "There's no need to eat them tonight. I've made you a huge goat dinner that will spoil by tomorrow."

"You're right," said the ogre, dropping the boy. "Let's fatten them up for a day or two." The good woman was glad at the chance to feed the boys a nice, warm meal. Later she took them to the bedroom where the ogre's daughters slept. There were seven ogresses, who all slept in one bed. Each one had tiny eyes, a pointy nose, a huge mouth full of sharp teeth, and a gold crown on her head. The woman placed the boys in a big bed next to the ogresses.

As his brothers slept, Thumbkin began to worry that the ogre might change his mind and kill them in their sleep. He looked over at the seven ogresses, and noticed again their crowns. Thumbkin quickly grabbed up his brothers' caps, and switched them for the crowns. Then he waited.

Sure enough, the ogre came in. He was sorry he hadn't made meat out of the boys earlier, so with a knife it his hand,

Thumbkin

he reached out in the dark and felt a crowned head. He went to the other side of the room and felt heads wearing caps. "Here they are," he muttered. "I almost got mixed up and killed my own terrible ogresses." He reached down and slit the throats of his seven daughters. Then, smiling with satisfaction, he returned to bed.

When Thumbkin heard the ogre's snore, he woke his brothers and told them to get dressed quietly. They quickly tiptoed out and ran away.

The next morning, the ogre went to collect his fresh meat. He went to the children's room and found his seven ogresses, as dead as could be. "Those rotten boys tricked me! They'll pay for this!"

The ogre threw on his magic traveling boots and ran out. He covered the countryside in only a few steps, and soon came to the road the boys had taken. They were very close to home when they saw the ogre approaching. He was stepping from hill to hill and jumping across large lakes as if they were small puddles.

Thumbkin spotted a little cave in a hill and quickly led his brothers into it. Along came the ogre, but he had grown tired from using the magical boots. He stopped to lie down, right by the entrance to the cave where Thumbkin and his brothers were hiding, and fell fast asleep.

Thumbkin told his brothers to run home, and that he would

Thumbkin

be there soon. Then he carefully removed the ogre's magical boots and put them on himself. He raced to the ogre's house and reported to the housekeeper that the ogre was in great danger. "Thieves have captured him," he said, "and they will kill him if they don't get all of his money. He asked me to fetch his sacks of gold."

The housekeeper brought out the riches, and Thumbkin hurried home with all the ogre's money. When the ogre awoke, he could not believe his magical boots were gone. He gave up searching for the boys, and journeyed back to his house, barefoot.

Thumbkin's family was overjoyed. They were filled with pride for the youngest son. "Thumbkin may be small," said his mother, "but he is very smart!!!" ✦

The Mountain and the Squirrel

by Ralph Waldo Emerson

The mountain and the squirrel
Had a quarrel;
And the former called the latter "Little Prig."
Bun replied,
"You are doubtless very big;
But all sorts of things and weather
Must be taken in together,
To make up a year
And a sphere.
And I think it no disgrace
To occupy my place.
If I'm not so large as you,
You are not so small as I,
And not half so spry,
I'll not deny you make
A very pretty squirrel track;
Talents differ; all is well and wisely put;
If I cannot carry forests on my back,
Neither can you crack a nut."

Thirty days hath September,
April, June, and November.
February has twenty-eight alone,
All the rest have thirty-one;
Excepting leap-year,
That's the time
When February's days are twenty-nine.

e Months

Growing Up

Time flies by so fast. With a little sunshine, water, and a lot of love, your grandchildren will sprout up before your eyes! The Body Collage is a fun and easy way to capture your grandchild's size and makeup at a particular age. When framed, it will make a great future gift to your grandchild, who will have long forgotten just how much his/her world revolved around Cheerios and dinosaurs! You and your grandchild will have great fun hunting for bits and pieces that reflect your grandchild's personality.

As you mark your grandchildren's height every year on your growth chart, you can marvel together at how much they've grown in the past year, look back at how cute and—hey! —short they were last year, and anticipate how much they will grow and change in the coming year.

BODY COLLAGE

Large paper bags or a large roll of kraft paper, markers, scissors, magazines, photographs, favorite things, glue

1. Cut open two large paper bags and tape them together until you have a size that's a little longer and a little wider than your grandchild. Or you can use a section of a kraft paper roll.

2. Have your grandchild lie on the paper. Trace around their outline. This is a great opportunity to tickle!

3. Cut out the body shape.

4. Flick through magazines together to find pictures of things your grandchild likes. These could be anything from pictures of animals to computer games, cars, or musical groups. You also can add candy wrappers, pieces of cereal boxes, stickers, photographs—anything you can find to represent your grandchild's favorite things. Cut them out and paste them to the body shape.

5. Ask your grandchild to draw his/her face, shoes, etc., using the markers.

6. Make sure to add your grandchild's age so you can record for posterity his/her favorite things at this age. Let dry.

GROWTH CHART

A roll of paper about 7 feet by 4 inches (adding-machine paper works well), tape, measuring tape or ruler, permanent markers, colored pencils, thumbtacks

1. Unroll the paper and tape down top and bottom edges to the floor. Place measuring tape on top of paper, slightly off center. Using permanent marker and measuring tape, draw a straight line down middle of paper and mark off inches and feet. Remove measuring tape.

2. Write "Our Growing Family" on the top. If you wish, let your grand-children decorate the chart with colored pencils. They can color every six inches with a different color. ("Grandma! I'm up to purple now!")

3. Tack the chart inside a closet door. Be sure the bottom of the chart touches the floor. (Alternatively, cut off the bottom 1 foot of the chart and position chart 1 foot above the floor.)

4. Using a different colored permanent marker, mark each grandchild's height and write the date. Holiday gatherings are the perfect time to update your chart every year

The Green Grass Grows All Around

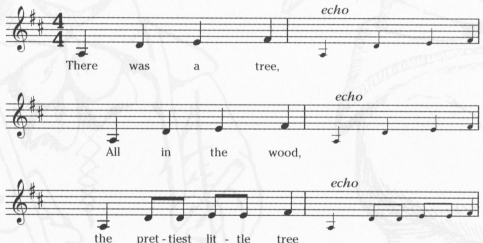

echo

There   was   a   tree,

echo

All   in   the   wood,

echo

the   pret - tiest   lit - tle   tree

echo

That   you   ev - er   did   see.

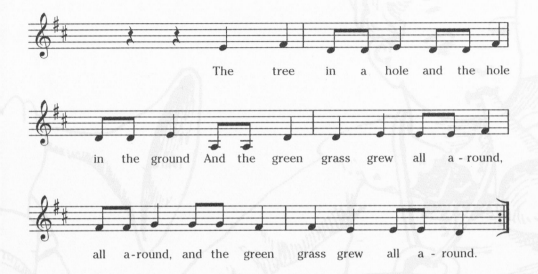

The tree in a hole and the hole in the ground And the green grass grew all a-round, all a-round, and the green grass grew all a-round.

2. And on that tree . . . there was a limb . . .
   The prettiest little limb . . .
        That you ever did see . . .
   The limb on the tree,
   And the tree in a hole,
   And the green grass grew all around,
        all around,
   And the green grass grew all around.

3. And on that limb... there was a branch...

4. And on that branch... there was a nest...

5. And in that nest... there was an egg...

6. And in that egg... there was a bird...

7. And on that bird... there was a wing...

8. And on that wing... there was a feather...

9. And on that feather... there was a bug...

10. And on that bug... there was a germ...

The Maid and Her Milk Pail

Once upon a time there was a young maid who was walking to the market with her pail of milk on her head. "This pail of milk will make me rich," she thought happily to herself. "I should be able to trade it for a half dozen eggs. And from the half dozen eggs, six chicks will be hatched. And when those six chicks are mostly grown, I should get a good price for them. I'll get the money in plenty of time to purchase a new dress for the May Day fair. I'll pick a green dress, as green is the color that suits me best. I'll go to the fair in my new green dress and be the envy of everyone there. Many young gentlemen will try to talk to me, but I'll just turn my head."

The young maid got so carried away that she quickly turned her head to match her daydream. Her pail of milk fell from her head, and the eggs, the chicks, the green gown, and all the dreams of what she would do at the May Day fair disappeared.

Don't count your chickens before they're hatched! ✦

Grandmother Says...

Practice makes perfect.

Live and learn.

Opportunity seldom
knocks twice.

As you make your bed,
so must you lie in it.

Actions speak louder than words.

Experience is the best teacher.

Make hay while the sun shines.

Always put your best
foot forward.

⊳⊶⊷⊶⊙⊶⊷⊶⊲

Where there's a will
there's a way.

⊳⊶⊷⊶⊙⊶⊷⊶⊲

As you sow, so shall you reap.

⊳⊶⊷⊶⊙⊶⊷⊶⊲

The first step is the hardest.

⊳⊶⊷⊶⊙⊶⊷⊶⊲

Never too old to learn.

⊳⊶⊷⊶⊙⊶⊷⊶⊲

Nothing ventured,
nothing gained.

⊳⊶⊷⊶⊙⊶⊷⊶⊲

You win some,
you lose some.

Ice Cream!

"**I** scream, you scream, we all scream for ice cream!" Sundaes, sandwiches, shakes, and sodas (sprinkles and whipped cream too)—grandchildren can have it all at Grandmother's house. Indulge little ones with these treats, and they will be clamoring to visit all the time.

BANANA SPLIT

1 banana
3 scoops favorite ice cream flavors (traditionally chocolate, vanilla, and strawberry)
1/2 cup chocolate fudge sauce
1 cup whipped cream *(see page 81)*
2 tablespoons chopped walnuts
1 maraschino cherry

1. Peel banana and slice it lengthwise. Place banana halves flat side up in the bottom of dish.

2. Add ice cream side by side on top of banana. Cover in chocolate sauce.

3. Garnish with whipped cream, nuts, and finally, the cherry on top!

Serves two or three.

HOT FUDGE SUNDAE

2 scoops of ice cream
1/2 cup chocolate fudge sauce
1/2 cup whipped cream *(see page 81)*
1 tablespoon chopped walnuts
1 maraschino cherry

1. Place two scoops of ice cream in deep bowl.

2. Layer fudge sauce, whipped cream, nuts and cherry on top. Serve immediately!

Serves one.

Ice Cream!

ICE-CREAM SANDWICHES

2 dozen chocolate chip cookies
  (see page 93)
1 gallon vanilla or chocolate ice cream,
  slightly softened
2 cups mini chocolate chips or sprinkles

1. Place and carefully flatten one scoop of ice cream on a cookie. Top with a second cookie and press down. Roll sides in chips or sprinkles. Place in a freezer bag and freeze immediately.

2. Allow sandwiches to freeze at least 2 hours before serving. Sandwiches will keep up to a week in freezer.

Makes twelve sandwiches.

BLACK-AND-WHITE MILKSHAKE

3 tablespoons chocolate syrup
1 cup milk
3 large scoops vanilla ice cream

1. Combine ingredients in a blender and blend on low until smooth and slightly foamy.

2. Serve immediately.

Serves two.

Variations: Try chocolate ice cream instead of vanilla for a chocolate shake, or use strawberry syrup and ice cream to make a strawberry shake, or substitute 1 tablespoon vanilla extract for the chocolate syrup to make a vanilla shake.

Ice Cream!

ICE-CREAM SODA

2 to 3 tablespoons chocolate or
    strawberry syrup
Chilled soda water
2 scoops ice cream
1 to 2 spoonfuls of whipped cream
    (optional)

1. Pour syrup into an 8-ounce soda glass and add soda water. Stir well until mixture is foaming at the top.
2. Add ice cream and top with whipped cream if desired.
3. Serve immediately with a straw and a long spoon.

Serves one.

Variation: substitute chilled root beer for the syrup and soda water mixture for a classic root-beer float.

WHIPPED CREAM

1/2 pint heavy cream
1 tablespoon vanilla extract
1 tablespoon white sugar

1. Combine ingredients in a large bowl and beat until stiff peaks form.
2. Serve immediately or cover and refrigerate for several hours until needed.

Makes two cups.

Little Cabin in The Wood

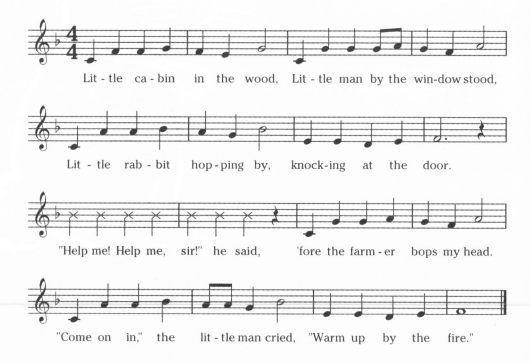

| Little cabin
In the wood, | Little man by the
Window stood, | Little rabbit
Hopping by, |

| Knocking
At the door. | "Help me! Help me, sir!"
He said, "fore the farmer... | ...Bops my
Head." |

| "Come on in,"
The little man cried, | "Warm up by the fire." |

Grandma and Bunny Brown

by Edith Roberts

B unny Brown was an only child, and the joy of his grandmother's heart. He was a fine lad, full of life and spirits, but he had one great fault: he never would pay attention to what he was doing. At school his master was always saying: "Now, Bunny Brown, don't stare about—look at the black-board!" or "Bunny Brown, look what you're doing or you'll tip that ink over!" But nothing cured Bunny of his carelessness, and the bottles of ink he upset and the suits of clothes he ruined caused endless trouble both at school and at home.

On his ninth birthday he grandmother gave him a scooter, which he soon learned to ride, and the next morning he started off to school on it in high spirits.

Grandma and Bunny Brown

"Now, Bunny dear," said Grandma Bunny, "you must look where you're going or you will have an accident."

"All right, Grandma," cried Bunny; "don't you worry!"

Then away he went at a great pace. At first he certainly did look where he was going; but soon he was turning his eyes in all directions, chiefly because he wanted to see if anyone was admiring the way he rode.

Now, just at the end of the hill there happened to be a small pile of stones in the middle of the road, and, as Bunny Brown did not see these, he allowed the wheel of his scooter to crash right into them. The next moment he found himself sitting on the ground with his cycle under him. He had never sat down so hard in his life before, and the shock brought the tears to his eyes. Then he began to yell so loudly that Grandma Bunny came running from her cottage.

Grandma and Bunny Brown

"Oh, what did I tell you, Bunny?" she cried. "You did not look where you were going!"

She helped him to get up, and dried his eyes, and he was sensible enough to own that it was his own fault, and that she was quite right.

It was some time before he sat down again with any pleasure, but his fall had taught him a lesson he did not forget.

"Ah, my little Bunny Brown," said his grandmother, "you will be saved many falls as you go through life if you look where you are going, and pay attention to what you are doing!"

"Yes, Grandma," he answered, "and I mean to do so."

Grandmother Says...

Faith will move mountains.

>—+—◄►—◦—◄►—+—◄

Honesty is the best policy.

>—+—◄►—◦—◄►—+—◄

Love will find a way.

>—+—◄►—◦—◄►—+—◄

One good turn deserves another.

>—+—◄►—◦—◄►—+—◄

Two wrongs do not make a right.

>—+—◄►—◦—◄►—+—◄

Those who live in glass houses should not throw stones.

>—+—◄►—◦—◄►—+—◄

You can't please everyone.

*It is no use crying over
spilt milk.*

*The grass is always greener
on the other side.*

*An ounce of prevention is
worth a pound of cure.*

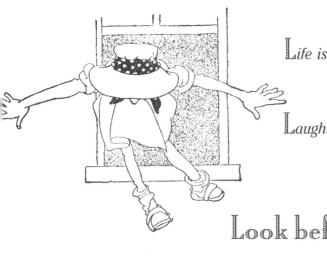

Life is just a bowl of cherries.

Laughter is the best medicine.

Look before you leap.

The Gingerbread Man

by Rowena Bennett

The gingerbread man gave a gingery shout:
"Quick! Open the oven and let me out!"
He stood up straight in his baking pan.
He jumped to the floor and away he ran.
"Catch me," he called, "if you can, can, can."

The gingerbread man met a cock and a pig
And a dog that was brown and twice as big
As himself. But he called to them all as he ran,
"You can't catch a runaway gingerbread man."

The gingerbread man met a reaper and a sower.
The gingerbread man met a thresher and mower;
But no matter how fast they scampered and ran
They couldn't catch up with a gingerbread man.

Then he came to a fox and he turned to face him.
He dared Old Reynard to follow and chase him;
But when he stepped under the fox's nose
Something happened. What do you s'pose?
The fox gave a snap. The fox gave a yawn,
And the gingerbread man was gone, gone, GONE.

Cookies and Treats

How does that cookie jar empty so fast? Well, it certainly can't be left that way! Keep baking these treats with care, and your grandchildren will never eat a cookie in their lives without reminiscing about their childhood in Granny's kitchen.

Cinnamon Sugar Cookies

1/2 cup butter (1 stick), room temperature
1/2 teaspoon salt
1 teaspoon grated lemon rind
1 1/4 cups sugar
2 eggs
2 tablespoons milk
2 cups flour
1 teaspoon baking powder
1/2 teaspoon baking soda
2 tablespoons ground cinnamon

1. Preheat oven to 400°F.
2. In a large mixing bowl, cream together butter, salt, lemon rind, and 1 cup sugar.
3. Add eggs and milk. Mix well.
4. In a separate bowl, combine flour, baking powder, and baking soda, and gradually add to the above mixture. Mix well.
5. Drop mixture onto greased cookie sheet, one rounded tablespoon at a time, 2 inches apart.
6. In a small bowl, mix 1/4 cup sugar and cinnamon.
7. Butter the bottom of a glass, dip into the cinnamon sugar mixture and flatten one cookie. Repeat until all cookies are flattened.
8. Bake 8 to 10 minutes until light golden.
9. Transfer cookies to wire racks and let cool.

Makes two and a half dozen cookies.

CHOCOLATE CHIP COOKIES

5 1/3 tablespoons butter,
    room temperature
1/2 cup sugar
1/4 cup packed brown sugar
1 egg
1 teaspoon vanilla extract
1 cup flour
1/2 teaspoon baking soda
1/2 teaspoon salt
1 cup semisweet chocolate chips

1. Preheat oven to 375°F.
2. In a large mixing bowl, cream together butter, white sugar, and brown sugar until light.
3. Add egg and vanilla. Mix well.
4. In a separate bowl, combine flour, baking soda, and salt, and gradually add to the above mixture. Mix well.
5. Add chocolate chips and mix well.
6. Drop mixture onto greased cookie sheet, one rounded tablespoon at a time, around 2 inches apart. (If using cookies for ice-cream sandwiches *(page 80)*, flatten dough slightly with back of spoon.) Bake 8 to 10 minutes until golden brown.
7. Transfer cookies to wire racks and let cool.

Makes about two dozen cookies.

MARSHMALLOW RICE TREATS

3 tablespoons unsalted butter
10 ounces mini-marshmallows
6 cups toasted rice cereal
1/2 cup chopped dried cranberries
1/2 cup chopped dried apricots

1. In a large stockpot, melt butter and marshmallows together.
2. Turn off heat and stir in cereal and dried fruits.
3. Spoon onto a 9" x 11" baking pan lined with wax paper. Flatten out using another piece of wax paper on top.
4. When cool, slice into 2-inch squares and store in sealed container.

Makes about two dozen treats.

TOUCH WOOD

All the children but the one dubbed "It" place themselves in various positions, each touching something that is wood. They then run from one wooden thing to another. "It" runs after them, and the first one he or she catches not touching wood becomes "It."

ROCKS, PAPER, SCISSORS

Two players face each other. Each extends a closed fist and says "Rock, paper, scissors." At "scissors" they turn their fists into one of the three objects: rock (a closed fist), paper (an open palm), or scissors (two fingers in a V shape). A rock wins by crushing scissors, scissors wins by cutting paper, paper wins by covering rock. The child with the higher-ranked hand shape wins or gets a point.

EGG AND SPOON RACE

Each child holds a spoon by its handle and places a hard-boiled egg on the spoon. With the spoon in one hand and without touching the egg to steady it, each child races to the finish line. If a child drops the egg, he or she must get the egg, return to the spot where egg dropped and continue to the finish line. First one to reach the finish line is the winner.

Easter EGGstravaganza!

*S*tash these eggheads around the house or garden and watch your grandchildren giggle gleefully as they uncover each funny face and race even faster to find candy-crammed eggs! Make your eggheads in advance as Easter gifts and then show your grandchildren how to plant their own earthy eggheads to personally grow, style, and decorate. (For more egg fun, see egg and spoon race on page 95.)

EARTHY EGGHEADS

Raw eggs, needle, markers, egg carton, grass seed, potting soil

1. Use a needle to make a hole about the size of a quarter in one end of an egg, then drain the egg and carefully rinse out the shell.

2. With the hole ends up, draw silly faces on the shells. Stand them in the carton.

3. Spoon soil into shells until they are 3/4 full. Sprinkle grass seed over the top. Add a bit of water and place in a sunny location.

4. Keep soil moist. Seeds should sprout in a few days and grass should start growing in about 10 days. Style each egghead of "hair"!

EDIBLE EGGHEADS

Raw eggs, needle, food coloring, water, bowls, small wrapped candies

1. Follow step 1 for Earthy Eggheads.

2. Mix favorite colors of food coloring with water in bowls. Dye eggs and let dry.

3. Carefully insert small-sized wrapped chocolates and candies into the shells.

Six Little Ducks

Six lit - tle ducks that I once knew,

Fat ones skin - ny ones, fair ones too, But the

one lit - tle duck with the feath - er on his back,

He led the oth - ers with a quack, quack, quack!

Six Little Ducks

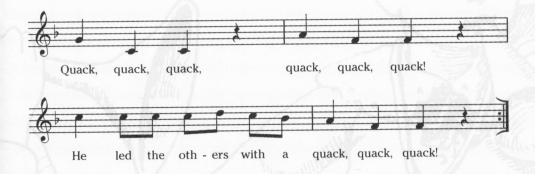

Quack, quack, quack,   quack, quack, quack!

He   led   the   oth - ers   with   a   quack, quack, quack!

2. Down to the river they would go,
   Wibble wobble, wibble wobble, to and fro,
   But the one little duck with the feather on his back,
   He led the others with a quack, quack, quack!
   Quack, quack, quack, quack, quack, quack!
   He led the others with a quack, quack, quack!

3. Home from the river they would come,
   Wibble wobble, wibble wobble, ho-hum-hum!
   But the one little duck with the feather on his back,
   He led the others with a quack, quack, quack!...

Ducklings Three

Anonymous

Flippy, and Floppy, and Flappy are three
Dear little ducklings that sail on the sea,
Sail in a tin, and a boot, and a box—
What do they care for the sharks or the rocks?
Hanky for sail and a skewer for mast,
Blown by the breezes they get along fast;
If one tips over it's nothing to him—
All little ducklings like fishes can swim.

The Wolf and
The Seven Little Kids

 nce upon a time there was an old mother goat who had seven young kids. She loved them all very much. One day, she needed to go into the forest to fetch some food. She called all seven of her children together and said, "Dear children, I must go into the forest this afternoon. I will be back by dinnertime. Please be careful not to let the dirty wolf inside. He likes to put on disguises, but don't let yourselves be fooled. You can always tell the wolf by his gruff voice and black paws."

The children told their mother not to worry, and she kissed them all good-bye.

Not long after, a knock came at the door. "Open up, dear children," called out the visitor. "It's your mother, and I've brought something back for each of you."

But the kids knew it was the wolf by his gruff voice. "Go

The Wolf and The Seven Little Kids

away," they cried. "You're not our mother. Her voice is soft and sweet. Yours is deep and gruff. You're the wolf!"

So the wolf went away to the shopkeeper and bought some chalk. He gobbled it up, and it made his voice soft. Then he returned, knocked at the door, and called out, "Open up, dear children. It's your mother, and I've brought something back for each of you."

But the wolf had put his black paw against the window, and so the children cried out, "Go away! You're not our mother. Her feet are small and white. Yours are big and black. You're the wolf!"

So the wolf went away to the baker. He told him that he had stubbed his toes, and that he needed some raw dough to soothe them. The baker covered the wolf's paws, and this made them white.

Then the villain went to the house for a third time, knocked, and called out, "Open up, dear children. It's your mother, and I've brought something back for each of you."

The kids called out, "First show us your paws so we know you are our dear mother."

He put his paw up to the window, and when they saw that it was white, they believed him and opened the door. And though they tried to find good hiding places, the wolf wasted no time in gobbling up one, two, three, four, five, six of the kids. He didn't know that number seven was hiding in the grandfather clock, so he went away, satisfied.

Soon after, the mother goat came home to find a hideous mess. The table was on its side, the chairs were scattered about, the bed was unmade, the oven door was open, and her children were nowhere to be found. She called out to them, each by name. It wasn't until she got to the seventh that she heard a peep. "Dear Mother, I'm in the clock case." She brought him out, and he told her that the wolf had come and gobbled up his brothers and sisters. She wept, but was determined to find that dirty scoundrel!

She stormed out the front door with her youngest by her side. They searched until they found the wolf, fast asleep under a tree. She looked at his bloated stomach and saw that something was squirming about inside. "Could it be that they are still alive?" she said. "Young One, run back to the house and fetch my scissors and a needle and thread. We're going to teach this beast a lesson."

So the youngest kid ran as fast as he could, and was back in no time. The mother goat cut the wolf's belly open, and out popped

The Wolf and The Seven Little Kids

one, two, three, four, five, six kids! They were all still alive and didn't have a single scratch. It seemed that in the wolf's haste to devour them, he had swallowed the kids whole. The mother goat was overjoyed, and she hugged and kissed them all. "Now go gather six large stones. We'll fill the monster's belly with them while he's still asleep." So that's what they did, and the mother goat sewed the wolf back up so quickly that he didn't even stir.

When the wolf had slept a long while, he woke up with an amazing thirst. He wanted to go to the well, but as he started to walk, the stones in his belly began to knock together. He cried out,

> What's that rumbling?
> My bones are crumbling.
> I thought I had eaten six little kids,
> But my tummy is full of stones, it is!

He finally reached the well, but as he leaned over to take a drink, the weight of the stones pulled him in. He sank to the bottom and drowned.

When the kids heard the news, they cried, "The wolf is dead! The wolf is dead!" and they danced with their mother around the well. ✦

Judge
not
by
looks
alone.

Little Red Riding Hood

Put on a puppet show of this favorite fairy tale with your grandchildren! (Parents can be the audience.) The puppets can be as elaborate as you and your grandchildren wish. You can substitute plastic spoons, permanent markers, glue, and felt in place of painting and sewing to simplify the spoon puppets. Alternatively, give Red a paper basket or dress up Grandma in lace, ribbons, and notions.

The script that follows can be simplified or added to. If there is only one little puppeteer, let him or her decide whether to be the Wolf or Red. You will easily be able to play all the other short parts. For young children, it may be enough to use just the two puppets and enact the scene between Red Riding Hood and the Wolf at Grandma's house. Good luck!

SPOON PUPPETS

Acrylic paints, paintbrush; two large wooden spoons; one small wooden spoon; colored yarn; glue; scissors; red, white, and green cloth; needle, thread

1. Paint Little Red Riding Hood's face onto the backside of the smaller wooden spoon. Paint Grandma's face with glasses and Hunter's face with mustache on the two larger spoons. (You can use plastic spoons and permanent markers instead.) Glue on different colored yarns for hair.

2. Cut three cloth circles about twice the length of the spoon handles: a smaller red circle for Red, white for Grandma, and green for Hunter. Cut a small hole in the middle of each circle. Slip each spoon handle through the appropriate-colored cloth. Use tape to fasten the underside of each cloth to its handle. (For Red, make and attach hood described in step 3 before completing step 2.)

3. Red's Hood: put two small pieces of red cloth on top of each other. Cut out a *D* shape slighter taller than the length of Red's spoon head. Sew together about ²/₃ of the curve of the *D* (the

bottom of the curve and the straight edge remain separate). Insert the bottom of *D* into the small circle in the middle of Red's cape. Open the hood's two bottom pieces and sew onto the underside of the cape.

4. Grandma's Cap: Cut a white circle about twice the width of Grandma's spoon head. Place some leftover fabric in the center of the circle and gather up the edge to form a pouch. Wrap a rubber band once or twice around it, just tight enough to hold in the stuffing but loose enough to fit around the top portion of Grandma's spoon head (you can use a ribbon to cover up the rubber band if you wish). Fluff out the frilly edge of Grandma's cap and adjust on Grandma's head. You will need to remove Grandma's cap and tape it onto the Wolf's head in the middle of the play. The little cap will look ridiculous on the Wolf, but that's part of the fun!

5. Hold spoon handles to move puppets. If you wish, cut two slits in the front and center of each cloth cape. The thumb and index fingers of your hand can go through the slits to become moveable puppet hands.

THE BIG, BAD WOLF

Brown sock, scissors, white felt, two white buttons (optional), glue, black felt or black button, brown felt, black or brown yarn

1. Pull the sock over your hand. Thrust your thumb into the heel section and your fingers into the toe section to form a mouth. Note where you will add teeth, eyes (where your knuckles are), nose, ears, and tail.

2. Cut triangular pieces of white felt for the big, bad wolf's sharp teeth—glue these to the edges of the mouth.

3. Glue or sew on white felt or white button eyes and a black felt or black button nose.

4. Glue on two large, brown felt triangles for ears; tufts of brown yarn for hair, and a long yarn tail.

Putting on the Show

NARRATOR

Once upon a time there was a lovely girl who wore her favorite hooded cape everywhere she went. Her nickname was Little Red Riding Hood, but sometimes "Red" for short. One sunny afternoon, Little Red Riding Hood's mother sent her to take a "get well" basket of chicken soup and crackers to her grandmother, who had a terrible cold. Her grandmother lived not far away, in a little cabin in the woods.

RED

I'm Little Red Riding Hood and I'm on my way to Grandma's house. Mom says I should go right to Grandma's house and not talk to strangers. And so here I go into the woods! (*Red skips through the woods and then stops suddenly.*)

RED

Oh! Look at those beautiful raspberries over there. I'll just stop for a little bit and pick some for Grandma.

WOLF (*in sweet voice*)

H-e-l-l-l-o-o, little girl!

RED

Oops! You scared me! I dropped all my raspberries!

WOLF

May I help you pick them up?

RED

Well, you look like a nice wolf, but I'm not allowed to talk to strangers.

WOLF

So I will just help and not talk to you.

RED

Oh, that's a good idea. (*They pick up berries for a while.*)

WOLF (*yawning*)

My, it's getting late! It's almost my bedtime.

RED

Oh no! I'm very late getting to Grandma's house. It's going to get dark soon! What am I going to do?

WOLF

Well, little girl, why don't you go this way? It's a shortcut.

RED

Thanks! (*Red goes off, but the shortcut is actually very long. The wolf tricked Red so he could get to Grandma's house first!*)

WOLF

Knock Knock!

GRANDMA
Who's there?

WOLF (*sweet tiny voice*)
It's Little Red Riding Hood!

GRANDMA
Come in, I've been waiting for you . . . !
AHHHH! A wolf!!

WOLF
Grrrrrr! Get over here! Get into the closet.
I'll eat you after I take care of Little Red
Riding Hood! And be quiet! Otherwise I'll
eat you both nice and slowly instead of in
one big bite! Oh, give me your cap! (*Wolf
puts on Grandma's cap and jumps into
bed. Little Red Riding Hood soon arrives.*)

RED
Granny, it's me, Little Red Riding Hood.
I've brought you some soup and fresh
berries to make you feel better.

WOLF
Come closer, so I can see you, child! You
know how bad my eyes are.

RED
Granny, what big eyes you have!

WOLF
The better to see you with, dear. Now
come closer.

RED
Granny, what big ears you have!

WOLF
The better to smell you with. Come just a
bit closer, dear.

RED
Oh Granny! What a BIG mouth you have!

WOLF
Grrr! Yes! The better to EAT YOU WITH!!!

RED
AAHHHHH! (*Wolf chases Red around.*)

RED
Help! Help! Help! (*A hunter who has been
out in the woods nearby hears the screams
and rushes to the cabin.*)

HUNTER
What's happening? Oh my! A wolf! *BANG!*
(*A very young child can be responsible for
this single exciting sound effect.*)

RED
Oh, thank you, thank you, thank you! But
where is my grandmother?

GRANDMA
Here I am! Let me out of here!

RED
Oh, Grandma! I'm so happy to see you! I
promise I will never ever talk to
strangers again. . . especially big, bad
wolf strangers!

THE END

Lenore's Chicken Potpie

Leonore is a grandmother with two recipes in this book and, if the truth be told, she probably should have her own cookbook altogether. She simply never makes anything that isn't high-end comfort food. Her chicken potpie is superb. She does make her own dough; however, to simplify life, I recommend you buy it frozen.

4 cups chicken broth
3 poached and cubed chicken breasts
4 to 5 cups cubed vegetables (any
    mixture of carrots, leeks, celery,
    mushrooms, pearl onions, zucchini,
    corn, green peas)
3 tablespoons butter
4 tablespoons flour
1 cup heavy cream
Salt and pepper to taste
9 oz. pastry dough
A little white flour for rolling out dough
1 egg

1. Preheat oven to 400°F.
2. Boil the chicken broth until it is reduced by half. Set aside.
3. Mix chicken and fresh vegetables and put in a baking dish.
4. Melt butter in a saucepan, add flour, and cook, whisking over medium-low heat, 2 to 3 minutes. Add broth. Cook, whisking, until thickened, another 3 to 4 minutes. Salt and pepper to taste and pour over chicken and vegetables.
5. On a lightly floured surface, roll the pastry out to form the shape of your baking dish, adding $1^{1}/2$" for an overlap.
6. Whisk egg. Brush the outside rim of baking dish with egg. Lay the pastry on top of dish and crimp around the edges. Use a fork to tamp down the edges, giving it a decorative look. Brush egg over the crust. Make a few small cuts in the crust for the steam to escape.
7. Bake for 20 minutes. Reduce heat to 375°F and bake another 15 to 20 minutes.

Serves four.

Little Red Caboose

by Deke Moffitt

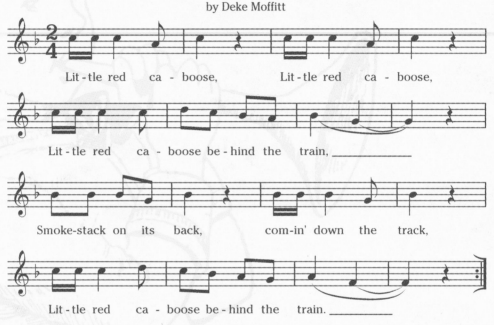

Lit - tle red ca - boose, Lit - tle red ca - boose,

Lit - tle red ca - boose be - hind the train, _____

Smoke-stack on its back, com-in' down the track,

Lit - tle red ca - boose be - hind the train. _____

2. Little red caboose,
Little red caboose,
Little red caboose behind the train,
Coming round the bend,
Hanging on the end,
Little red caboose behind the train.

The Peanut Song

Oh, a peanut sat
On a railroad track,

His heart was all a-flutter.

Along came the five-fifteen,

Uh-oh, peanut butter!

Round and Round

Round and round
The garden, like a
Teddy bear.

One step . . .

Two step . . .

And tickle under there!

The Shower
by Catherine A. Morin

One day, as they all scampered home from
    their school, the Pixies—*and* Polly,
It started to rain, and poor Polly—oh, dear!—
    had forgotten her brolly!

"Hooray!" cried the Pixies, "*we* don't need
    umbrellas; ho! isn't this jolly!"
Each crept 'neath a stool, leaving Polly in the rain
    feeling quite melancholy.

Classic Drinks

Grandma always needs a few refreshing and tummy-warming drinks up her sleeve. Start with favorites like lemonade and iced tea, and then impress them with Shirley Temple, a sweet cocktail to make grandchildren feel grown up. On chilly days, warm up little ones with steamy cups of delicious hot chocolate or hot apple cider.

OLD-FASHIONED LEMONADE

1 cup water
2 cups white sugar
Juice of six lemons (1 1/2 cups)
8 cups cold water
1/4 cup sweetened cranberry juice optional
Ice cubes
2 lemons sliced thin and halved
3 or 4 sprigs fresh mint leaves

1. In a medium-sized saucepan, combine 1 cup water and 2 cups sugar. Boil on low, stirring constantly, until sugar is completely dissolved, for about 5 minutes. Remove from heat.

2. When syrup has cooled (approximately 10 minutes), add lemon juice and stir well.

3. In a large pitcher, combine sugar and lemon syrup with 8 cups cold water. For pink lemonade, add the cranberry juice.

4. Serve lemonade over ice. Garnish with lemon slices and mint.

Serves six to eight.

SHIRLEY TEMPLE

Ice cubes
1 tablespoon maraschino cherry syrup
1 to 2 cups ginger ale
1 maraschino cherry

1. Fill an 8-ounce soda glass with ice, add syrup and ginger ale, and stir.

2. Garnish with cherry and serve immediately.

Serves one.

Iced Sun Tea

4 tea bags
8 cups cold water
2 lemons, sliced thin and halved
Ice cubes
Sugar

1. Combine water and tea bags in large pitcher. Place in a sunny spot and allow to sit for up to six hours.

2. Remove from sun, stir well, and remove tea bags. Serve over ice with lemon slices to garnish. Sweeten to taste.

Serves six.

Mulled Apple Cider

1 quart (8 cups) apple cider
Peel from 1/2 orange
1 1-inch peeled and sliced fresh ginger
1 teaspoon whole allspice
6 cinnamon sticks
Additional cinnamon sticks, one per cup
   (Kids love to try to use them as straws!)

1. Put juice or cider in a large saucepan over the lowest heat.

2. Wrap up the remaining ingredients in a big piece of cheesecloth and put it into the pot, or put them in a strainer that hooks over the pot. Simmer at the lowest heat for 1 1/2 to 2 hours.

3. Throw away the spices, pour the cider into mugs, and add a cinnamon stick.

Serves six.

Hot Chocolate

Whole milk (skim milk or water may be substituted)
Unsweetened cocoa
Sugar
Mini-marshmallows
Peppermint sticks
Whipped cream *(see page 81)*

1. Following portion directions on cocoa packaging, combine milk and cocoa in a medium-size saucepan on low heat.

2. Whisk the mixture as it heats until blended. Mixture should be warm but not boiling. Add sugar and continue to blend until hot.

3. Serve with marshmallows, whipped cream, and a peppermint stick.

Independence Day

It's the Fourth of July, and time to celebrate America's independence! Let the rockets glare and trumpets blare! Let your little ones have their own parade with star crowns, flags, and firework streamers.

STARS AND STRIPES CROWN

Scissors, white and blue construction paper, red yarn, paper glue or paste, pencil, silver glitter, stapler

1. Cut a band of white paper 3 inches wide and long enough to fit around child's head.

2. Cut seven pieces of yarn the length of the white band. Glue the first piece of yarn to top edge of band. Glue rest of yarn $1/2$ inch apart to form the thirteen stripes of the flag.

3. Cut a 3- by 4-inch rectangle of blue paper and glue to middle of band.

4. Use a pencil to mark fifty dots on the blue rectangle: nine rows, alternating six dots and five dots per row.

5. Place a dab of glue on each pencil mark. Sprinkle glitter over glue, let dry, and shake off excess.

6. Fit crown to child's head and staple ends of band together.

PAPER FLAG

Rectangular sheet of white paper, red and blue construction paper, scissors, paper glue or paste, pencil, silver glitter, newspaper, tape

1. Cut seven strips of red paper and glue onto white paper.

2. Cut small blue rectangle and glue to top left corner.

3. Follow steps 4 and 5 of Stars and Stripes Crown.

4. Take a large sheet of newspaper and fold in half. Start at one corner and roll tightly into a long stick shape. Tape securely.

5. Attach flag to top.

Variation: Tape red, white, and blue crepe-paper streamers to end of newspaper rolled into stick for a fireworks baton.

★ ★ ★ ★ ★ ★ ★ ★ ★ ★

The Grand Old

Oh the grand old Duke of York,
He had ten thousand men;
He marched them up the hill,
And marched them down again.

Now when they were up, they were up,
And when they were down, they were down,
And when they were only halfway up,
They were neither up nor down.

Duke of York

The Bremen Town Musicians

nce upon a time there was a donkey who had served his master for many long years. But the donkey had grown tired and weak. One day, the master climbed up on the donkey's back with five big bags of grain to sell in town. Well, this was just too much for the poor old donkey. He fell to his knees with a thud.

"AAAHHHHH!" cried the master as he flew over the donkey's head and landed flat on his face in the dirt. "You no-good donkey!" he hollered. "I'll sell you to the butcher for this!" And the master marched back to the house to take care of his smashed nose.

The sad donkey started moaning low and long. Then he let out some short, high-pitched brays: Hee-haw! Hee-haw! Hee-haw! A wise crow flew down from his nearby perch. "Donkey, why don't you run away? Go to the town of Bremen! They need musicians. With your musical moans and brays you'll be a fine one!"

The Bremen Town Musicians

The donkey thanked the crow and went off as quickly as his worn-out legs would carry him. After trotting some distance, the donkey saw a dog by the road, barking loudly. "What's the matter, Dog?" asked the donkey.

"I'm old and can't hunt anymore. I ran away from my master because he was going to get rid of me."

"Come with me, Dog. Your bark is still strong, you'll find work in Bremen."

The dog thanked the donkey, and the two were off to Bremen. After walking for a while, the donkey and the dog saw a cat by the road, meowing softly. "What's the matter, Cat?" asked the donkey.

"I'm old and can't catch mice anymore. I ran away from my mistress because she was going to drown me."

"Come with us, Cat. Your meow is still pleasing, you'll find work in Bremen."

The cat thanked the donkey, and now the three of them were off to Bremen. After walking for a while, the donkey, dog, and cat saw a rooster by the road, crowing with all his might. "What's the matter, Rooster?" asked the donkey.

The Bremen Town Musicians

"I'm old and can't tell time anymore. I ran away from my mistress because she was going to cook me."

"Come with us, Rooster. Your crow is still hearty, you'll find work in Bremen."

The rooster thanked the donkey, and now the four were off to Bremen. But Bremen was still far away, and it was getting dark. The group decided to stop and sleep by the edge of a forest. The donkey and dog curled up beneath a big tree. The cat climbed up to rest in its branches. And the rooster flew to the very top of the tree. Before settling down, he looked all around. Deep in the forest, he saw a faint light. "Hey! I think there might be a house in this forest!" he called down to the others.

"Maybe there's food," said the dog. So the four went into the forest in search of food and better shelter. They walked and walked until they found the brightly lit cottage. The donkey, the largest of the four friends, approached the nearest window and looked inside.

"What do you see?" asked the rooster from below.

"I see a table with a meal fit for a king, and the biggest, ugliest and meanest-looking bunch of thieves around it," said the donkey.

At the mention of the food, the dog jumped on the donkey's

The Bremen Town Musicians

back for a better view. The cat jumped on top of the dog, and then the cock flew up on top of the cat. The weight was too much for the donkey and he fell to his knees. WOOOFFFF! MEEOOOW! GAAAAK! screamed the dog, cat, and rooster as they went flying over the donkey's head and crashed through the window.

Startled by the noise and the scary shapes hurtling through the air, the thieves sprang from their seats and ran as fast as they could out the door. "Hooray!" cheered the donkey as he helped his friends up from the floor. The four happily gobbled up all the wonderful food left on the table.

"Finally, a good night's rest on full tummies!" said the donkey. He found a bed of straw in the yard. The dog lay down on a rug by the back door. The cat curled up by the warm fire. The rooster perched next to the nice, warm chimney on the roof.

Sometime after midnight, the thieves noticed the light had gone down in the cottage. Cold and hungry, the leader of the band ordered one of his men to go back and inspect it. The chosen bandit reluctantly did as he was told. He quietly entered the cottage and found a candle. The sleeping cat heard a noise and opened her eyes, which the bandit thought were coals from the fire. He quickly approached the two lights to light the candle.

The Bremen Town Musicians

The cat was not amused to have a candle stuck toward her eyes. She leaped at the thief's face, hissing and scratching. The thief screamed in terror. He ran toward the back door, stepping on the dog, who quickly chomped at his leg. The thief untangled himself and ran across the yard, straight into the back end of the donkey, who immediately gave him a swift kick. The rooster woke up from all the noise and screamed Cock-a-doodle-doo!

The thief picked himself up and ran away as fast as he could, back to his band. "There is a wicked witch by the fire who clawed at my face with her long nails," he reported to his leader. "Then a growling man by the door stabbed me in the leg with a knife, a monster in the yard hit me in the chest with a huge stick, and a judge on the roof screamed down, "Bring me that scoundrel!"

After hearing this spine-chilling story, the thieves decided never to return to their hideout. As for the four friends, they decided that the cottage suited them just fine. Now and then, they would put on a concert for the nearby forest animals: Hee-haw! Woof, ruff, bow-wow! Meow, meow! Cock-a-doodle-doo! The forest animals all agreed that even though the group was old, they were very fine musicians. ✦

MUSICAL CHAIRS

Someone needs to control the music. Chairs are placed in two rows, back to back, one less in number than the players, who then gallop round them in time to the music. Suddenly the music stops, and everybody tries to sit in a chair. Whoever doesn't get a chair is then out of the game. A chair is removed and the game continues until only one player, the winner, is left.

LONDON BRIDGE

Two children clasp hands and raise them to form an arch or "bridge." The rest of the players walk under the bridge one by one, singing:

> London Bridge is falling down, falling down, falling down.
> London Bridge is falling down, my fair lady!

When they sing "my fair lady," the bridge drops and traps someone in their arms. They begin rocking the trapped child in their arms singing:

> Take a key and lock her up, lock her up, lock her up.
> Take a key and lock her up, my fair lady!

The trapped child then replaces one of the children forming the bridge and the game continues.

BLIND MAN'S BUFF

One child is blindfolded with a handkerchief so that he or she cannot see, and is placed in the middle of a small, fairly empty room. The other children turn her around three times, and she tries to catch anyone she can. The other children need to call out to help her. The one caught has to be the next "blind man."

I Know an Old Lady

Anonymous

I know an old lady who swallowed a fly.
I don't know why she swallowed a fly.
Perhaps she'll die.

I know an old lady who swallowed a spider.
It squirmed and wriggled and turned inside her.
She swallowed the spider to catch the fly.
I don't know why she swallowed a fly.
Perhaps she'll die.

I know an old lady who swallowed a bird.
How absurd! She swallowed a bird.
She swallowed the bird to catch the spider,
She swallowed the spider to catch the fly,
I don't know why she swallowed a fly.
Perhaps she'll die.

I know an old lady who swallowed a cat.
Think of that! She swallowed a cat.
She swallowed the cat to catch the bird,
She swallowed the bird to catch the spider,

She swallowed the spider to catch the fly.
I don't know why she swallowed a fly.
Perhaps she'll die.

I know an old lady who swallowed a dog.
She went the whole hog when she swallowed the dog.
She swallowed the dog to catch the cat,
She swallowed the cat to catch the bird,
She swallowed the bird to catch the spider,
She swallowed the spider to catch the fly,
I don't know why she swallowed a fly.
Perhaps she'll die.

I know an old lady who swallowed a cow.
I don't know how she swallowed the cow.
She swallowed the cow to catch the dog,
She swallowed the dog to catch the cat,
She swallowed the cat to catch the bird,
She swallowed the bird to catch the spider,
She swallowed the spider to catch the fly,
I don't know why she swallowed a fly.
Perhaps she'll die.

I know an old lady who swallowed a horse....
She's alive and well, of course!

Pot Roast

My friend Lenore's mother served this to me recently at a dinner party. She is a great-grandmother and this is one of her most requested recipes. Serve with small steamed red potatoes, fettucini, or mashed potatoes. It will satisfy your entire family.

2 to 3 tablespoons vegetable oil
2 large yellow onions, diced
2 to 3 crushed garlic cloves (optional)
2 1/2 to 3 lbs. lean beef brisket
Salt & pepper (to taste)
1 cup boiling water
1 large can plum tomatoes, crushed
6 medium-size potatoes, peeled and quartered
4 to 6 large carrots, peeled and quartered
Several handfuls fresh green peas or
   1 package frozen (optional)

1. Heat oil in a Dutch oven or large stockpot.
2. Add diced onion and brown lightly. Add garlic and sauté for 1 to 2 minutes.
3. Add meat and brown on all sides over high heat, around 6 to 7 minutes. Add salt and pepper. Reduce heat and add boiling water. Cover pot tightly.
4. Simmer on low heat for 45 minutes.
5. Add crushed tomatoes, cover again, and simmer while preparing vegetables.
6. Stir vegetables into pot.
7. After meat has cooked a total of 2 hours, remove it carefully and lay it on a board. Slice thinly.
8. Return meat to pot and simmer 1 hour, until everything is soft and tender.
9. During the last 1/2 hour you may add fresh peas or defrosted peas.

Serves four to six.

Sour Cream Spinach Casserole

Kelly is not yet a grandmother, but her eight-year-old daughter Saxon told me this is her mom's best recipe, so I have got to believe that when Saxon has children it will be at the top of her list. Kelly believes in cooking with organic ingredients, and serves this every Thanksgiving with her turkey.

1 10-oz. bag frozen chopped spinach
1/2 bag garden herb croutons (about 2 1/2 cups)
1 1/4 cups sour cream
1 packet onion soup mix
1 1/4 tablespoons melted butter

1. Put frozen spinach in a fine strainer over a bowl to drain and defrost. After 2 to 3 hours, when spinach is defrosted, press out the excess liquid with a spoon.
2. Preheat oven to 350°F.
3. Crush croutons in a plastic bag with a rolling pin or skillet until they are closer to the consistency of bread crumbs.
4. Mix spinach, sour cream, and onion soup in a large bowl.
5. Transfer to a small casserole dish and spread out evenly.
6. Flatten the top and pour the crushed croutons evenly over the surface.
7. Drizzle butter with a spoon evenly over the croutons.
8. Cover with a lid (or aluminum foil) and bake for 1/2 hour, until croutons are a light golden brown.

Serves four as a side dish.

Advice to Small Children

by Edward Anthony

Eat no green apples
  or you'll droop,
Be careful not
  to get the croup,
Avoid the chicken-pox
  and such,
And don't fall out
  of windows much.

Boom, Boom, Ain't It Great to be Crazy

A horse and a flea and three blind mice

Sat on a curb - stone shoot - ing dice, The

horse he slipped and fell on the flea,

"Whoops," said the flea, "There's a horse on me!"

Chorus

Boom, boom, ain't it great to be cra - zy, Boom,

boom, ain't it great to be cra - zy,

Gid - dy and fool - ish the whole day through, Boom,

boom, ain't it great to be cra - zy?

2. Way down South where bananas grow,
   A flea stepped on an elephant's toe,
   The elephant cried with tears in his eyes,
   "Why don't you pick o someone your size?"

   Chorus

3. Way up North where there's ice and snow,
   There lived a penguin and his name was Joe,
   He got so tired of black and white,
   He wore pink slacks to the dance last night.

   Chorus

141

Old Mother Hubbard
Went to the cupboard,
To give her poor dog a bone;
But when she got there
The cupboard was bare,
And so the poor dog had none.

Rapunzel

nce upon a time there was a couple who dreamed of having a child. Finally, their prayers were answered and they happily awaited the birth of their baby. Now, this couple lived in a house that overlooked the loveliest garden, which was surrounded by a high wall. No one dared to enter this garden, for it belonged to an evil sorceress.

One day, the woman looked down into the garden and saw a bed full of the finest rapunzel lettuce. The leaves looked so fresh and green that she longed to eat them. Day by day, as she waited for her child to be born, her craving grew until she couldn't stand it. "If I don't get some of that rapunzel, I will certainly die," she moaned to her husband.

Her husband loved her dearly and was determined to help her. At dusk, he climbed over the wall and dropped into the sorceress's garden. He quickly gathered some rapunzel and returned to his wife. It tasted so good that she desperately wanted more.

Rapunzel

So at dusk the next day, her husband set off to fetch her more rapunzel. Over the wall he went, but when he reached the other side he drew back in fear. Standing before him was the evil sorceress herself. "How dare you climb into my garden and steal my lettuce?" she said, with an angry stare. "You will pay for this!"

"Oh!" he pleaded, "I beg your pardon, but I had to come. My wife saw your rapunzel from our window, and thought that she'd rather die than not have some. I came to get it to save both she and our unborn child."

The sorceress's anger quickly faded, and a smile crept across her face. "If what you say is true, then you may take as much rapunzel as you wish, on one condition: Your newborn shall be mine!"

The man had no choice but to agree, and as soon as the child was born the sorceress appeared to claim her. She named her Rapunzel, and took her away.

When the girl reached the age of twelve, the sorceress locked her in a tower in the middle of the forest. The tower had no stairs or doors, but only a small window near the very top. When the sorceress wished to get in, she stood down below and called out,

Rapunzel

> Rapunzel, Rapunzel,
> Let down your hair.

Rapunzel would unpin her long, golden braids and let them fall down from the window. The sorceress used the braids to climb the sixty-foot wall of the tower. She always left before dark, and lonely Rapunzel would sing herself to sleep.

One evening, a prince was riding through the forest and happened to pass by the tower. Upon hearing Rapunzel's sweet song, he stopped and listened. The prince longed to see the woman whose voice was so delightful, but he could not find the tower door. He returned to the tower every day to listen to the enchanting song. One day, the prince arrived earlier than usual and did not hear any singing; so he stretched out under the shade of a tree to wait. Soon the sorceress approached, and the prince heard her call out,

> Rapunzel, Rapunzel,
> Let down your hair.

Rapunzel

Rapunzel let down her braids, and the sorceress climbed up the tower.

"So that's how it's done," said the prince. "Then I too will visit the songbird."

The following evening, the prince went to the foot of the tower and cried,

> Rapunzel, Rapunzel,
> Let down your hair.

As soon as she had let down her braids, the prince climbed up to her. At first Rapunzel was terribly frightened, for she had never seen a man before. But the prince spoke gently, and told her that her singing had touched his heart. Very soon Rapunzel forgot her fear, and when he asked her to marry him, she agreed at once. "Yes, I will gladly go with you, only it will take some work for me to get down out of the tower. Every night when you come, bring me a spool of silk thread. I will weave a strong ladder, and when it is finished I will climb down."

Rapunzel

The sorceress, of course, knew nothing of their plan, until one day, Rapunzel accidentally turned to her and said, "Why are you so much heavier than my prince? It takes no time at all for him to reach me. He always reaches me in a moment."

"Oh, you wicked child!" cried the sorceress. "I thought I had hidden you safely from the world, and yet you have managed to deceive me."

In her rage, she grabbed Rapunzel's beautiful hair, wound it around her wrist, and snipped it off with a pair of scissors. The sorceress then took Rapunzel to a deserted place, and left her to die.

That night, the sorceress fastened the braids to a hook on the tower window. The prince came and called out,

Rapunzel, Rapunzel,
Let down your hair.

The sorceress let down the braids, and the prince climbed up as usual. But instead of his dear Rapunzel, he found the sorceress, who screamed, "Aha! You thought you'd find your beloved, but the pretty bird is gone from this nest, and her song is done. The cat caught the bird, and will scratch your eyes out too."

The prince was beside himself with grief, and in his despair

Rapunzel

he jumped down from the tower. He escaped with his life, but the thorns he fell into pierced his eyes. Blind and miserable, he wandered through the forest for some years, as unhappy as he could be. At last he came to the deserted place where Rapunzel was living. Suddenly the prince heard a voice that lifted his heart up. He ran toward the sound, and when he was quite close, Rapunzel recognized him. Weeping, she ran to embrace him. Two of her tears touched his eyes, and in a moment he could see as well as ever. He led her to his kingdom, where they were received and welcomed with great joy. They had a beautiful wedding and they lived happily ever after. ✦

The Tale of Custard the Dragon
by Ogden Nash

Belinda lived in a little white house,
With a little black kitten and a little gray mouse,
And a little yellow dog and a little red wagon,
And a realio, trulio, little pet dragon.

Now the name of the little black kitten was Ink,
And the little gray mouse, she called her Blink,
And the little yellow dog was sharp as Mustard,
But the dragon was a coward, and she called him Custard.

Custard the dragon had big sharp teeth,
And spikes on top of him and scales underneath,
Mouth like a fireplace, chimney for a nose,
And realio, trulio daggers on his toes.

Belinda was as brave as a barrel full of bears,
And Ink and Blink chased lions down the stairs,
Mustard was as brave as a tiger in a rage,
But Custard cried for a nice safe cage.

Belinda tickled him, she tickled him unmerciful,
Ink, Blink and Mustard, they rudely called him Percival,
They all sat laughing in the little red wagon
At the realio, trulio, cowardly dragon.

Belinda giggled till she shook the house,
And blink said *Weeek!,* which is giggling for a mouse,
Ink and Mustard rudely asked his age,
When Custard cried for a nice safe cage.

Suddenly, suddenly they heard a nasty sound,
And Mustard growled, and they all looked around.
Meowch! cried Ink, and Ooh! cried Belinda,
For there was a pirate, climbing in the winda.

Pistol in his left hand, pistol in his right,
And he held in his teeth a cutlass bright;
His beard was black, one leg was wood.
It was clear that the pirate meant no good.

Belinda paled, and she cried Help! Help!
But Mustard fled with a terrified yelp,
Ink trickled down to the bottom of the household,
And little mouse Blink strategically mouseholed.

But up jumped Custard, snorting like an engine,
Clashed his tail like irons in a dungeon,
With a clatter and a clank and a jangling squirm
He went at the pirate like a robin at a worm.

The pirate gaped at Belinda's dragon,
And gulped some grog from his pocket flagon,
He fired two bullets, but they didn't hit,
And Custard gobbled him, every bit.

Belinda embraced him, Mustard licked him;
No one mourned for his pirate victim.
Ink and Blink in glee did gyrate
Around the dragon that ate the pyrate.

Belinda still lives in her little white house,
With her little black kitten and her little gray mouse,
And her little yellow dog and her little red wagon,
And her realio, trulio, little pet dragon.

Belinda is as brave as a barrel full of bears,
And Ink and Blink chase lions down the stairs,
Mustard is as brave as a tiger in a rage,
But Custard keeps crying for a nice safe cage.

Halloween

*C*hildren love Halloween because of the candy, of course, and because of all the spooky *fun! Let them decorate your house with creepy things and play a hilarious game or two.*

PIPE CLEANER SPIDERS

Black pipe cleaners, string

1. Twist pipe cleaners together to form round bodies with eight legs each.

2. Attach string and hang from doorframe to about top-of-head height. Scatter little ones around house.

FINGERPRINT SHAPES

Black inkpad, paper, markers, glue, glitter, scissors

1. Let children make as many Halloween shapes as they can come up with using fingerprints and markers. Add glowing eyes with dabs of glue and glitter. Cut out shapes to decorate house.

Some suggestions:
Spider: thumbprint; draw on legs.
Cat: pinky print for head, thumbprint for body; draw on ears, tail, and legs.
Owl: pinky print for head, thumbprint for body; draw on ears and claw feet.
Bat: thumbprint; draw on wings.

THE MUMMY GAME

Rolls of cheap toilet paper

1. Whoever is chosen to be the mummy stands with arms and legs apart.

2. Wrap up the mummy with toilet paper!

3. Mummy chases the other children (arms front, legs straight, clumps around and moans). Yikes!

TUB OF WORMS

Cooked spaghetti, oil, plastic tub, wrapped candy, several peeled whole grapes, baby carrots, blindfold (optional)

1. Prepare tub before children arrive. Mix spaghetti with a bit of oil to get things slimy. Add wrapped candy, grapes, and carrots.

2. Children feel around the "worms" to find treats. Do not pull out anything that feels like eyeballs and fingers!

Jell-O, Jell-O Everywhere

Jell-O, Jell-O everywhere, it's so fun to eat! Did you know they start as packets, those cubes I love so sweet? So easy-peasy, it's really swell, add some water and stir it well. Presto, magic-there's plenty for Granny and me!

1 cup boiling water
2 packages (8-serving size) Jell-O®
    brand gelatin, any flavor
1 cup cold fruit juice
Ice cubes
Fruit (mandarin orange or banana slices,
    or chopped berries), optional

1. In a large bowl, empty gelatin into boiling water and stir at least 2 minutes, until completely dissolved.
2. Mix cold juice with ice cubes to make 1 1/2 cups. Add juice to gelatin mixture, stirring until slightly thickened. Remove any remaining ice.
3. Pour into 13" x 9" pan. Refrigerate at least 1 hour or until firm. If desired, add fruit after 20 minutes. Dip bottom of pan in warm water for about 15 seconds. Cut into 1-inch squares or use cookie cutters for fun shapes. Lift from pan.

Serves 8.

FRUIT PARFAITS

Follow steps 1 and 2. Slice 1 cup berries and divide among 6 dessert glasses. Divide 3/4 cup gelatin into glasses and refrigerate about 45 minutes, until just set but not firm. Stir 3/4 cup whipped cream *(page 81)* into remaining gelatin until smooth and add to glasses. Refrigerate another hour until firm. Garnish with berries on top.

TIPS AND IDEAS

- Use plastic cups, Dixie cups, a cupcake pan, or ice-cube tray for small servings.
- Replace all of the water called for with fruit juice, syrup from canned fruit, or carbonated soft drinks for extra flavor.
- To layer different colored gelatins, chill each layer until set but not firm before adding the next layer. The additional gelatin mixtures must be cool and slightly thickened before layering.
- Try adding gummy candies in place of fruit! Gummy worms like green jello and gummy fish like blue!

Little Baby

Dance, little Baby, dance up high!
Never mind, Baby, Grandma is by.

Crow and caper, caper and crow,
There, little Baby, there you go!

Up to the ceiling, down to the ground,
Backwards and forwards, round
and round;

Dance, little Baby, and Grandma will sing,
With the merry coral, ding, ding, ding!

Twelve Dancing Princesses

Once upon a time there was a king who had twelve beautiful daughters. The princesses slept side by side in twelve beds. Each night when they went to bed, the king shut and locked their door. But each morning he opened the door to find that their shoes had been danced to pieces, and nobody could explain how it happened.

So the king announced that anyone who discovered where the princesses secretly danced in the night could choose one of them to be his wife and would inherit the kingdom. But whoever tried and failed to make the discovery after three days and nights would be put to death.

A prince soon appeared and offered to take the risk. At night, he was taken to the chamber next to the one where the princesses slept in their twelve beds. The doors of both chambers were left open so that the princesses could not leave without being seen. But the prince's eyes grew heavy, and he fell asleep on his watch.

Twelve Dancing Princesses

When he woke in the morning, all the princesses had been dancing. The soles of their shoes were full of holes. The second and third evenings passed with the same result, and the prince lost his head. Many others came after him and offered to take the chance, but they all lost their lives.

One day, an old soldier passed through the kingdom. On his travels he met an old woman who asked him where he was going. "I hardly know myself," said the soldier, and added jokingly, "I'd like to discover where the twelve princesses dance, and become king."

"Well, that's not very hard to do," said the old woman. "Don't drink any of the wine the princesses serve in the evening. Then, as soon as they leave you, pretend to be fast asleep."

The old woman gave him a cloak and said, "When you wear this, you will be invisible. Follow the princesses wherever they go." Once the soldier heard all this good advice, he was determined to try his luck.

He was welcomed into the castle, and when the evening came he was led to the outer chamber. Just as he was going to lie down, the eldest of the princesses brought him a cup of wine. The soldier had tied a sponge beneath his chin, and he let the wine run into it. He didn't drink a drop. Then he lay down on his bed, and in a little while began to snore very loudly. When the twelve princesses heard this they laughed, and the eldest said, "This fellow, too, might have done better things with his life!" They groomed themselves in front of their mirrors, and skipped about, eager to begin dancing.

Sure that they were quite safe, the eldest went up to her own bed and clapped her hands, and the bed sunk into the floor. The soldier saw them going down through the opening one after another, the eldest leading the way. With no time to lose, he jumped up, put on the invisible cloak, and followed them. But in the middle of the stairs he stepped on the corner of the youngest princess's dress, causing her to cry out to her sisters, "Someone grabbed at my dress."

"You silly creature!" said the eldest. "You caught it on a nail." Then down they all went, and at the bottom they found themselves in a most delightful orchard. The leaves on the trees were silver, and glittered and sparkled. The soldier wished to take away some token of the place; so he broke off a little branch. Snap!

"Did you hear that noise?" asked the youngest sister. "Something is terribly wrong."

Twelve Dancing Princesses

"It is only our princes, who are shouting for joy at our approach," said the eldest.

Then they came to another orchard, where all the leaves on the trees were gold; and afterward to a third, where the leaves were all glittering diamonds. The soldier broke a branch from each; and every time there was a loud noise, which made the youngest sister tremble with fear. Snap! Crack! But the eldest still said it was only the princes, who were crying for joy. So they went on until they came to a great lake; and at the side of the lake were twelve little boats with twelve handsome princes in them.

The princesses got into their boats, and the soldier stepped into the same boat with the youngest. As they were rowing over the lake, her prince said, "I don't understand it, but the boat seems much heavier today.

"It is only the heavy heat," said the princess.

On the other side of the lake stood a beautiful, brightly lit palace. When the boats landed, everyone rushed up the palace steps. Each prince danced with his princess, and the invisible soldier danced among them; and when any of the princesses had a cup of wine set by her, he drank it all up, so that when she put the cup to her mouth it was empty. At this, too, the youngest sister was

Twelve Dancing Princesses

horribly frightened, but the eldest always silenced her. They danced until three o'clock in the morning, and then all their shoes were worn out. So, the princes rowed them back over the lake; but this time the soldier placed himself in the boat with the eldest princess. On the opposite shore, the princesses said good-bye to their princes.

As they approached the staircase, the soldier quickly ran ahead to his room and lay down. The sisters heard the soldier snoring in his bed. They said, "We are safe." In the morning, the soldier said nothing about what had happened. He wanted to see more of this strange adventure, and went again the second and third nights. Everything happened just as before; however, on the third night,

the soldier carried away one of the golden cups as a token of where he had been.

Finally, the soldier was taken before the king to tell what he knew. He brought the three branches and the golden cup. The king asked him where his twelve daughters danced at night. The soldier told the king all that had happened and showed him the three branches and the golden cup. The king called for the princesses, and asked them if what the soldier said was true. They confessed, and the king asked the soldier which daughter he would choose for his wife. He answered, "I am not very young, so I will have the eldest."

They were married that very day, and the soldier was chosen to be the king's successor.

Pretty (and Yummy) Things

*T*each your grandchildren about the joy of giving. Encourage them to make two friendship bracelets—one to keep and one to give. Granddaughters will love the felt flower chain, which can be adapted to make a necklace, bracelet, or belt. And the sweet necklace is so yummy even grandsons will enjoy making one (or two) to snack on.

FELT FLOWER CHAIN

marker, felt, scissors, stapler, glue,
long strip of ribbon

1. Draw simple flower shapes onto felt and cut out. Flowers should be at least an inch wide.

2. Cut out centers for the flowers from the leftover scraps—they can be simple circles, stars, or smaller flower shapes. Shapes should be about 1/2 inch wide.

3. Staple flowers onto the ribbon, keeping the ends of the staples on the flower side.

4. Glue the flower centers onto the flowers, covering the staple ends. (If you wish to make smaller flowers with smaller centers, use needle and thread to stitch onto ribbon instead of stapling.)

FRIENDSHIP BRACELET

11/2 feet suede cord, three beads, scissors

1. Cut the cord into three 2-inch pieces and two 6-inch pieces.

2. Use one 6-inch piece to tie together the three short pieces.

3. Braid together the three short pieces for a bit, slide a bead onto the middle lace, and repeat with remaining cord and two beads.

4. Tie off with remaining 6-inch cord. Approximate the length required to tie around little wrists and trim off excess.

SWEET JEWELRY

Cheerios, Fruit Loops, Apple Jacks
cereal, long licorice strips

1. String the cereal onto the licorice. Tie the ends together, wear, and eat!

An Elegant Tea Party

Gather your family together for a delicious tea party. Brew a bracing pot of tea or make iced tea or lemonade *(page 120)*. These wonderful scones are an old family recipe from Great-grandma Coughlan. To complete your menu, add fresh fruit, little cucumber and butter sandwiches (thinly slice peeled cucumber and bread, and remove crust from bread), lemon squares *(page 28)*, cookies *(page 92)*, and jams *(page 271)*. For an extra special tea, why not make strawberry shortcake *(page 54)*! With a cup of tea in hand and good things to eat, you can relax, chat , enjoy your family, and savor a lovely afternoon.

NANA'S SCONES

1 1/2 cups white flour
1/2 cup whole wheat flour
1/3 cup granulated sugar
1 tablespoon baking powder
6 tablespoons chilled, unsalted butter
1/3 cup baking raisins
1/2 cups heavy whipping cream
2 large eggs, beaten

1. Preheat oven to 375°F.
2. In a large bowl, combine all-purpose and wheat flour, sugar, and baking powder.
3. Using a pastry blender or two knives scissor fashion, cut in the butter until the mixture resembles course crumbs. Stir in the raisins, mixing well.
4. Combine heavy cream, reserving 1 tablespoon, and 1 beaten egg in a small bowl. Add to flour mixture. Stir until just moistened. Do not over mix.
5. Transfer the dough to a lightly floured surface and knead gently. Roll or pat the dough into a circle about 7 inches round and 1 1/2 inches thick.
6. Lightly flour the rim of a glass and press into dough, making perfect rounds. Repeat until all dough is used. Place the scones on an ungreased cookie sheet.
7. Whisk egg and 1 tablespoon heavy cream. Brush egg mixture over scones.
8. Bake for approximately 15 to 20 minutes, or until lightly browned.
9. These are especially delicious when served warm with butter and preserves.

Makes six scones.

The Fox and The Grapes

Once upon a time there was a fox who wandered about the countryside drinking freely from the streams and eating the wealth of food that was to be found. But recently, a drought had made food and water more difficult to find. The fox was forced to travel beyond the land he knew in order to find food. He spent many long, hot days searching for something to eat.

Finally, he came to a lush orchard. There he found rows and rows of grapes growing high on their vines, which had been trained over tall branches. He stopped at a particularly tasty-looking bunch ripening on a vine. "Wow! What luck!" said the fox. "Those grapes are just the thing to both feed my hunger and quench my thirst on this hot summer's day."

The fox jumped up to reach for the grapes, but he could not get high enough. He took a few steps back to try again. With a running start, the fox jumped up into the air, but he still didn't get

The Fox and The Grapes

high enough. Returning to his starting spot, he tried again. He almost got high enough this time, but not quite. He tried and tried, again and again, but just couldn't get high enough to grab the grapes.

Finally, he had to give up. As he walked away, he put his nose in the air and said, "I am sure those were sour grapes."

It is easy to reject what you cannot have. ✦

Try, Try Again

by T. H. Palmer

'Tis a lesson you should heed,
   Try, try again;
If at first you don't succeed,
   Try, try again;
Then your courage should appear,
For, if you will persevere,
You will conquer, never fear;
   Try, try again.

Making Special Friends

*E*verybody needs a friend, and a little stuffed bear or doll often becomes an inseparable one for young children. Follow the steps below to make a beanbag bear or little girl doll. Your grandchildren will enjoy watching and helping their special friend come to life with a few snips and stitches. Substitute felt shapes for buttons and scraps of fabric for the beans if the doll is for a very young child.

BEANBAG BEAR OR DOLL

Scrap of felt or other fabric, needle, thread, buttons, yarn, dried beans

1. Fold your sheet of fabric in half and pin at the edges to hold.

2. Draw a teddy bear or gingerbread figure outline on the fabric and cut it out.

3. Sew two large buttons for eyes and a smaller button nose to the face on the front of one of your pieces of fabric. Stitch on a small piece of yarn for the mouth. A bear's mouth can be a little rounded W shape. A little girl's mouth can be heart-shaped. If you are not going to add clothing to your doll, sew two or three buttons onto the chest.

4. Let your grandchild name the doll. You can embroider the name (or your grandchild's name) to the back.

5. Place the two pieces of fabric together, front sides facing each other. Sew edges together, leaving a large opening for the beans. Take care to keep the stitches close together so that the dried beans won't slip out. If you are making a little girl with yarn hair, fold long pieces of yarn in half and place them between the two fabric pieces at the top of the head. Leave about 1/2 inch of yarn sticking out, and sew edges of fabric tight.

6. Turn the doll right side out. Stuff a generous amount of beans into the doll and sew the opening closed.

7. For a bear, make a little vest if you wish. For a girl doll, trim the front pieces of yarn shorter for bangs and make her a little dress, simple apron, or skirt.

The Bear Went over the Mountain

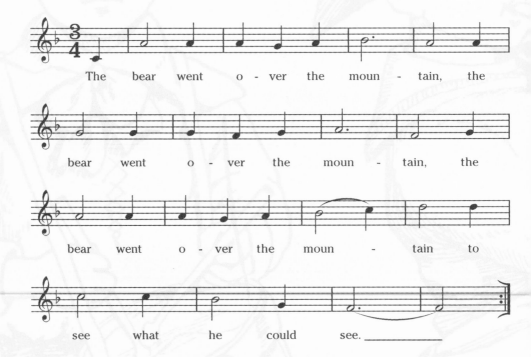

The bear went o - ver the moun - tain, the
bear went o - ver the moun - tain, the
bear went o - ver the moun - tain to
see what he could see. _____

Tingalayo

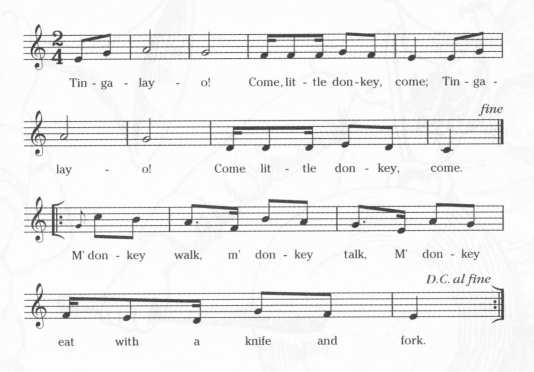

Tin - ga - lay - o! Come, lit - tle don - key, come; Tin - ga -

lay - o! Come lit - tle don - key, come.

fine

M' don - key walk, m' don - key talk, M' don - key

D.C. al fine

eat with a knife and fork.

The Man, His Son, and His Donkey

nce upon a time, a man and his son decided to sell their donkey at a fair in the neighboring town. The three had not walked far when they passed a group of young girls who were standing around a well. One girl said, "Look at those silly fools. They let their donkey set the pace, while they march by its side. Why don't they ride to town?" The man heard this remark, and not wanting to be thought of as a silly fool, he placed his son on the donkey's back

They had not gone much farther when they passed a little country inn, where a group of old men were talking together outside. "There," said one of the men. "That just proves what I was saying; the young have no respect for the old. Look at that young boy riding without a care in the world, while his father has

The Man, His Son, and His Donkey

to walk by his side. Get down, you brat, and let your father ride awhile!" Well, the boy was truly his father's son: He didn't like anyone calling him names. So he jumped down from the donkey and insisted that his father take his place.

They continued on this way for a while until they came across a group of women, each with a child on her hip. "Isn't that just like a man?" One woman sneered. "He sits up there like he's the king, while his poor son can hardly keep up!" The man and his son glanced at each other sheepishly. Then the man pulled his son up to sit by his side.

They rode this way until they were almost to town, and met up with a young man who said, "Pardon my asking, but is that your donkey?" The man told him that it was, and the young man frowned. He said, "If that were my donkey, I would not overload his back like that. You and your son appear to be healthy and strong. You could as easily carry your donkey as make him carry you." The man and his son felt embarrassed that they had been so selfish. They

The Man, His Son, and His Donkey

immediately jumped down off the donkey, found a pole to balance the animal on, and carried the donkey that way until they got to the town bridge.

A small crowd of young boys and girls had gathered to watch the donkey being carried by its masters. They began to laugh loudly, as they had never seen such a strange sight. The noise startled the donkey so that he kicked himself free of the pole. The unfortunate animal fell into the stream and sank. Well, the man and his son could do nothing but return home, poorer than when they'd started. On the way home the man told his son, "If we try to please everyone, we please no one." ✦

Grandmother Says...

The best things in life are free.

>—I—◆>—O—<◆—I—<

Beauty is only skin deep.

>—I—◆>—O—<◆—I—<

All that glitters is not gold.

>—I—◆>—O—<◆—I—<

Don't put all your eggs in one basket.

>—I—◆>—O—<◆—I—<

Never judge by appearances.

Money does not grow on trees.

*Things are not always
what they seem.*

*You can't tell a book
by its cover.*

*Don't go near the water until
you learn how to swim.*

Waste not, want not.

A penny saved is a penny earned.

The Little Turtle

by Vachel Lindsay

There was a little turtle.
He lived in a box.
He swam in a puddle.
He climbed on the rocks.

He snapped at a mosquito.
He snapped at a flea.
He snapped at a minnow.
And he snapped at me.

He caught the mosquito.
He caught the flea.
He caught the minnow.
But he didn't catch me.

Here is the Church

Here is the church.

Here is the steeple.

Open the doors.

And see all the people.

My Turtle

This is my turtle.
He lives in a shell.
He likes his home very well.

He pokes his head out
When he wants to eat.

And he pulls it back
When he wants to sleep.

The Little Mermaid

nce upon a time, there was a little mermaid who lived far out to sea, where the water is the darkest blue and so deep that no anchor can touch the bottom. She wasn't just any girl with a fish tail; she was the daughter of the sea king, and the granddaughter of the noble queen mother. Nevertheless this mermaid ,who had so much to be thankful for— good friends, loving sisters, a wonderful father, a doting grandmother, and all the treasures you could imagine—was really quite miserable.

Ever since her grandmother had first told her stories about the great ships upon the surface of the sea, she had longed to know more about the lives of the humans: What did they look like? Were they like her? What did they do for adventure? Her grandmother, too, had been very curious about the "upper world" in her youth. She tried her best

The Little Mermaid

to paint a full picture of human life for her youngest granddaughter. But the little mermaid's father thought the surface was a dangerous place, and made her promise not to go there until after her fifteenth birthday.

Well, one day she quite forgot her promise, and swam up to the sunlight. She came up close to a sailing ship. Careful not to be noticed, she spied on the people aboard. Among the passengers was a handsome prince. The little mermaid fell in love with him at first sight.

Suddenly a storm broke out, and the ship was violently tossed on the waves. The crew was forced to jump overboard, and the prince struggled to stay afloat. Without hesitation, the little mermaid swam to him and pulled him to the nearest shore, next to his castle. Wanting to make sure he was all right, she waited in the surf, out of sight. When he awoke, he saw a beautiful woman standing over him. Thinking she was the one who saved him, he smiled at her. Well, it turns out she was a princess, and the prince asked her to be his wife. They were to be married in a week.

The Little Mermaid

The little mermaid was heartbroken. She swam down to her
father's kingdom as fast as she could. But since she was not
allowed to go to the surface, she dared not tell anyone in her
family about what had happened—not even her beloved
grandmother. The next day, she visited the dreadful sea
witch and asked for her help. "I know what you have
come for, my pretty," said the witch. "If you agree
to leave your tongue behind, then I will grant
your wish." The little mermaid agreed.
"Well," snorted the witch, "you can't expect to
win the prince's heart wearing those fins."
Legs magically appeared where the little
mermaid's tail had been. "I will give you
three days to make him fall in love with you.
If you should fail, I will melt you into foam,"
the sea witch cackled. "Your soul will be lost
forever!" The little mermaid sped up to the
surface, for she could no longer breathe as a fish.

She swam back to the shore where she had left the prince. He
was walking on the beach with his dog when he spotted her. She
seemed familiar to him, but he could not remember where they

The Little Mermaid

had met. And the little mermaid couldn't tell him that it was she who saved him from the shipwreck because she no longer had her voice. So they just smiled at each other, and he invited her to stay at his castle. As the days passed, he grew very fond of the little mermaid, but he was already engaged to the woman he thought had saved him.

When the week was through, the prince married the princess, and the little mermaid returned to the shore and waited to be turned to foam. Instead, she saw her sisters in the surf. They had all lost their hair. They had sold it to the sea witch in exchange for the little mermaid's life. Her oldest sister gave her a tiny dagger and told her she must stab the prince through the heart while he slept. Then she would regain her tail and become a mermaid again.

That night, the little mermaid went to the wedding ship where the prince and princess slept. She bent over their bed, and gave them each a tender kiss. She glanced down at the gruesome

The Little Mermaid

dagger she held, and threw it into the sea. Then she jumped overboard, and immediately turned to foam. It appeared that the sea witch's curse had come to pass after all, and that the little mermaid's soul was lost forever.

But a wonderful thing happened. The sun's rays warmed the foam and lifted it up to the sky. The little mermaid's loving nature and the unselfishness of her deed caused her to float into paradise. She became one of the spirits of the air who watch over all the little children of the world. If you look very carefully, you just might see her sitting on a cloud or sliding down a rainbow. ✦

Ladybird

Ladybird, ladybird, fly away home!

Your house is on fire,
your children all gone,

All but one, and her name is Ann,

And she crept under the pudding pan.

Baby Beluga

Words and Music by Raffi

Ba - by be - lu - ga in the deep blue sea,

swim so wild and you swim so free.

Hea - ven a - bove and the sea be - low And a

last time to Coda

lit - tle white whale on the go.

Ba - by be - lu - ga, oh, ba - by be - lu - ga,

Is the wa - ter warm? Is your ma - ma home with

you so hap - py?

Coda

go; _____ You're just a lit - tle white whale on the go.

2. Way down yonder where the dolphins play,
   Where you dive and splash all day
   Waves roll in and the waves roll out.
   See the water squirtin' out of your spout.

   Baby beluga, oh baby beluga,
   Sing your little song; sing for all your friends.
   We like to hear you.

3. When it's dark, you're home and fed,
   Curl up snug in your water bed
   Moon is shining and the stars are out.
   Good night, little whale, good night.

   Baby beluga, oh baby beluga,
   With tomorrow's sun, another day's begun.
   You'll soon be waking.

Learn to enjoy the little things—
there are so many of them.

—Anonymous

The Fisherman and His Wife

nce upon a time there was a fisherman who lived with his wife in a shack by the sea. One day he was sitting fishing by the clear water. Suddenly, he felt a big tug on his line, and when he pulled it up, there was a great fish on his hook. "Please let me live," the fish pleaded. "I am not really a fish. I am an enchanted prince."

"I want nothing to do with a fish that can talk," said the fisherman. "Swim away as fast as you please." So he put it back, and the fish darted straight down to the bottom.

When the fisherman returned home to his wife, he told her all about the great fish.

"Didn't you make a wish before letting him go?" asked his wife.

"No," said the fisherman. "What should I have wished for?"

"Ah!" said his wife. "We are so poor, living in this old, dirty shack. Go back and ask for a little cottage."

The fisherman did not like the idea of going, but he also did

The Fisherman and His Wife

not like arguing with his wife. When he got to the sea, the water
had turned yellowish green. He stood at the water's edge and said,

> Fishy, fishy in the sea,
> If you're a man, then speak to me.
> Though I don't like my wife's request,
> I've come to ask it nonetheless.

Then the great fish came swimming to him and asked, "What
does your wife desire?"

"Ah," said the fisherman, "my wife says that I should have
asked you for something before I let you go. She does not like
living in a shack, and wants a little cottage."

"Go, then," said the fish. "It is done."

So the man went home to find his wife standing at the door of
a cozy cottage. "Come in, come in," she called.
"Isn't this better than the shack?" The rooms
were comfortable and clean, and behind the
cottage there was a little garden with all
sorts of flowers and fruit trees.

"Ah!" said the fisherman. "How happy
we shall be."

The Fisherman and His Wife

"We will try," said his wife.

Everything went well for about a week, and then the wife said, "Husband, this cottage is too cramped, and the garden is a great deal too small; I want to live in a large stone castle. Go to the fish again, and tell him to give us a castle."

"But Wife," said the fisherman, "I don't like to go to him again. We should be happy with the cottage."

"Nonsense!" said the wife. "It is easy for him to do. Go ask him."

The fisherman went, but his heart was very heavy. When he reached the sea, it looked dark purple and gloomy. He went close to it, and said,

> Fishy, fishy in the sea,
> If you're a man, then speak to me.
> Though I don't like my wife's request,
> I've come to ask it nonetheless.

"Well, what does she want now?" said the fish.

"Ah!" said the man, "My wife wants to live in a stone castle."

"Go home," said the fish. "It is done."

So the fisherman returned home and found his wife standing before a great castle. She took him by the hand as they entered.

The Fisherman and His Wife

The rooms were full of golden chairs and tables; and behind the castle was a wooded area half a mile long, full of sheep, and goats, and hares, and deer; and in the courtyard were stables for horses and cows and the finest carriages. "Well," said the fisherman, "now we will live contented and happy in this beautiful castle for the rest of our lives."

"Perhaps," said the wife. "But let us consider and sleep on it before we make up our minds." So they went to bed.

The next morning, the wife woke up at daybreak and saw the glorious countryside through her window. Her husband yawned, so she poked him with her elbow. "Get up, Husband," she said. "We must rule over all the land. I want us to be king and queen."

"Wife, Wife," said the fisherman, "why should I wish to be king? I will not be king."

"Husband," she said, "say no more about it, just go and try. I shall be queen!" So the man went away, but he was nervous. The sea looked a dark gray, and was covered with foam as he cried out,

> Fishy, fishy in the sea,
> If you're a man, then speak to me.
> Though I don't like my wife's request,
> I've come to ask it nonetheless.

The Fisherman and His Wife

"Well, what does she want now?" said the fish.

"Great fish," said the fisherman, "my wife wants us to be king and queen."

"Go home," said the fish. "It is done."

Then the fisherman went home. As he came close to the palace, he saw a troop of soldiers and heard the sound of drums and trumpets. When he entered, he saw his wife sitting on a high throne of gold and diamonds, with a golden crown upon her head. "Ah, Wife!" said the fisherman. "What a fine thing it is to be king and queen! Now we shall never have anything more to wish for."

"I don't know about that," she said. "Never is a long time. I am queen, it's true, but I should be pope. Go to the fish, and ask him to make me pope."

"Oh, Wife, Wife!" he said, "How can you be pope? There is but one pope at a time in Christendom. The fish cannot make you pope."

"What nonsense!" she said, "If he can make a king, he can make a pope. Go and try him."

So the fisherman went. But when he came to the shore the wind and sea were raging, and the ships danced upon the hazardous waves. The fisherman was terribly frightened, and

209

The Fisherman and His Wife

trembled, so that his knees knocked together. But he went to the shore and said,

> Fishy, fishy in the sea,
> If you're a man, then speak to me.
> Though I don't like my wife's request,
> I've come to ask it nonetheless.

"What does she want now?" said the fish.

"Ah!" said the fisherman. "She wants to be pope."

"Go home," said the fish. "It is done."

Then the fisherman went home and found his wife sitting on a throne that was two miles high; and she had three great crowns on her head. Many bishops and priests stood around her, and on either side there were two rows of burning lights of all sizes. "Well, Wife," said the fisherman, "it is a grand thing to be pope; and now you must be content, for you can be nothing greater."

"We'll see," said the wife. Then they went to bed, but the fisherman's wife could not sleep all night for thinking what she should be next. At last morning came and the sun rose. "Ha!" she whispered as she looked through the window. "I must have the

The Fisherman and His Wife

power to rule the sun!" She woke her husband, and said, "Husband, go to the fish and tell him I want to be Lord of the sun and moon." The fisherman was half asleep, but the thought terrified him so much that he fell out of bed.

"Oh, Wife!" he said, "isn't being pope enough?"

"No," she said, "I am very uneasy, and cannot bear to see the sun and moon rise without my permission. Go to the fish quickly."

The fisherman was trembling with fear; and as he was going down to the shore a dreadful storm arose, so that the trees and the rocks shook; and the heavens became black, and the lightning struck, and the thunder rolled; and the fisherman said,

> Fishy, fishy in the sea,
> If you're a man, then speak to me.
> Though I don't like my wife's request,
> I've come to ask it nonetheless.

"What does she want now?" said the fish.

"Ah!" said the fisherman. "She wants to be Lord of the sun and moon."

"Go home," said the fish, "to your shack again!"

And there they live in their old, dirty shack to this very day. ✦

One, two, three

One, two, three, four, five,
Once I caught a fish alive.
Six, seven, eight, nine, ten,
But I let it go again.
Why did you let it go?
Because it bit my finger so.
Which finger did it bite?
The little one upon the right.

Picture Perfect: Frames

Is there any better way to display all of those pictures of your grandchildren than in frames they helped you create? Decoupage is the art of decorating with paper cutouts. It is a simple technique and can be used to decorate everything from shoeboxes to furniture.

Next time you take your grandchildren to the beach, bring a little beach home with you to decorate a frame. (Don't forget to take photographs of your day of fun in the sun with the children.)

DECOUPAGE FRAME

old magazines and greeting cards, scissors, water, plastic bowl, Elmer's glue, paintbrush, plain wood picture frame

1. Go through used magazines and old greeting cards with your grandchildren to find and cut out pictures you like.

2. Pour a small amount of water into a plastic bowl and slowly add glue, stirring constantly until the mixture is a soupy consistency.

3. Use a paintbrush to spread some of the mixture onto a small area of the frame. Apply cutouts to this area, over-lapping to cover completely.

4. Add more glue mixture to another area of the frame and continue in this fashion until the entire wood area of the frame is covered. Apply a thin coat of glue mixture to the entire area to seal the pictures in permanently and create a clear glaze when dry. Leave to dry.

SEASHELL FRAME

Water, plastic bowl, glue, paintbrush, plain lucite or glass frame, sand, seashells

1. Mix glue with water as for decoupage frame. Spread mixture all around the edge of frame—don't worry about making it even.

2. Lay frame faceup and sprinkle sand on top of the glue. Shake off excess sand and then glue seashells along the bottom edge of frame. Leave to dry.

3. Insert a photograph from your day at the beach with your grandchildren.

Picture Perfect: Games

Kids love to look at themselves. With these activities your grandchildren will be so busy looking for matching pictures of themselves and trying to reassemble the puzzle that they won't realize they are enhancing their concentration skills and beefing up their memory muscles! Good going, Grandma!

MEMORY GAME

Camera with film, scissors

1. Photograph your grandchildren, their favorite toys, and other family members (don't forget the family pet). Have two sets of prints made.

2. Cut all the pictures to uniform size, trimming matching pictures in the same way. Round off corners.

3. Shuffle the "deck" and then spread the photos facedown on a tabletop.

4. Have each child turn up one card and then another, in search of a matching pair, turning up two cards at a time. If they have different pictures, they're flipped facedown again. If a match, the photos are removed from the board. The game continues until all matching pairs have been found.

PICTURE PUZZLE

Camera with film, glue, posterboard, scissors

1. Take a photo of your grandchild or grandchildren together and have it developed as a 5- by 7-inch (or larger) photograph.

2. Enlist the little ones to help you glue the photo to a posterboard.

3. After the glue is dry, cut the picture into lots of fun shapes. Mix up the pieces on top of the table.

4. Hey presto! You have a picture puzzle. For a little added fun, write a little note, like "Grandma loves you," on the back of the photograph before you cut it up. The kids can flip the pieces over and assemble the word puzzle to find the hidden message!

Stone Soup

nce upon a time there was a great famine, which swept the land. Villagers desperately guarded their food, hiding it away from their friends and neighbors. One day, a peddler came through the village looking to trade his goods for something to eat. But the villagers quickly informed him that there was not a bite of food to be found for miles.

"Well," he said, "that's no problem. I'll just make some stone soup to share with all of you." Out of his wagon he pulled a large iron kettle and filled it with water he had gotten from a stream a few hours back. Next he pulled three smooth stones out of a velvet bag, and dropped them into the water.

Soon, more people gathered to see what was happening. "I'm making stone soup," announced the peddler. "Stick around and have some."

"Stone soup? Hmmm ... I have some cabbage in my cellar," offered one villager. "Would it taste good with the stones?"

Stone Soup

"Of course," said the peddler. "There's nothing better than stone and cabbage soup." So the villager went off to fetch the cabbage.

"Well, I think I have a little cured ham," offered the butcher. "Would that help the flavor?"

"You bet it would," said the peddler. "Bring it on out." So the butcher went off to fetch the ham.

"I may have a few potatoes," offered another villager. "Would you like them for the soup?"

"That would be just great!" said the peddler. "Potatoes are the perfect addition."

So it went, with the villagers offering all sorts of ingredients, such as carrots, onions, beans, herbs, and so on, until a delicious meal was ready for all to enjoy. After everyone had had their fill of the wonderful soup, the villagers asked the peddler if he might sell his magical stones. He replied, "I am sorry, but there is no amount of money that could persuade me to part with my stones." So the villagers had to content themselves with what he had given them. They thanked the peddler and sent him on his way. But from that time on, well after the famine was over, they talked about the finest soup they had ever tasted. ✦

If You're Happy

If you're hap-py and you know it, clap your hands. (clap, clap)   If you're

hap - py and you know it, clap your hands. (clap,   clap)   If you're

hap - py and you know it, then your   face will sure - ly show it.   If you're

hap - py and you know it clap your hands. (clap,   clap)

2. ...stomp your feet (stomp, stomp)...

3. ...shout hurray (Hurray!)...

4. ...do all three (clap, clap, stomp, stomp, hurray!)...

Momma Bread

My high-school girlfriend, Pleasant Coggershall, baked the best bread I ever had. My own children yearned for it ever since they tasted it, and so I've made it every Thanksgiving for many years. I make enough to freeze, give away, toast for breakfast, and make sandwiches with stuffing, turkey, lingonberries, and gravy the day after Thanksgiving. Yum.

4 cups lukewarm water
1 tablespoon sugar
3 packages active dry yeast
3/4 lb. (3 sticks) butter, melted
3 tablespoons kosher salt
1/2 cup honey
1/4 to 1/2 cup of molasses
5 eggs (room temperature)
3 lbs. whole wheat flour (9 cups)
2 lbs. unbleached white flour (6 cups)

1. Empty yeast into 2 cups of water in a large bowl and add sugar. Set aside in a warmish place for 15 to 20 minutes, until foamy.
2. Add, in the following order—stirring as you go—butter, salt, honey, molasses, eggs, 2 cups of water, and the whole-wheat flour. Mix.
3. Add the white flour (reserving about 1 cup for kneading), and mix again. Let stand for 10 minutes.
4. Transfer the dough to a lightly floured surface and knead at least 10 to 15 minutes. If the dough is sticky, sprinkle it lightly with flour as you work.
5. Butter a large bowl. Turn the dough in the butter to coat. Cover loosely with a warm, damp dishtowel and set aside in a warmish place to rise for 1 1/2 to 2 hours. Punch it down and let it rise again (1/2 hour or so.)
6. Preheat oven to 450°F. Butter five 9" x 5" x 3" loaf pans or two cookie trays.
7. Transfer the dough to a lightly floured surface. Cut into five pieces. Knead each, shaping it into a loaf. Press loaves into prepared pans or put on trays. Cover again and let them rise 1/2 hour.
8. Bake all the loaves together at 450°F for 10 minutes. Turn heat down to 350°F. Bake until bread is golden brown (another 20 to 30 minutes). Remove loaves from pans and let cool.

Makes five loaves.

First Thanksgiving of All
by Nancy Byrd Turner

Peace and Mercy and Jonathan,
And Patience (very small),
Stood by the table giving thanks
The first Thanksgiving of all.
There was very little for them to eat,
Nothing special and nothing sweet;
Only bread and a little broth,
And a bit of fruit (and no tablecloth);
But Peace and Mercy and Jonathan
And Patience, in a row,
Stood up and asked a blessing on
Thanksgiving, long ago.
Thankful they were their ship had come
Safely across the sea;
Thankful they were for hearth and home,
And kin and company;
They were glad of broth to go with their bread,
Glad their apples were round and red,
Glad of mayflowers they would bring
Out of the woods again next spring.
So Peace and Mercy and Jonathan,
And Patience (very small),
Stood up gratefully giving thanks
The first Thanksgiving of all.

Marbles

Young children (but not so young that marbles would be a choking hazard) can play a simplified version of Ring Taw, the most popular marble game during settler times. Draw a ring on the ground and place several marbles inside. Children practice shooting a marble from outside the ring, trying to knock other marbles out of the ring. Older children can play against each other "for keeps," keeping marbles they knock out. The one with the most marbles wins.

TIDDLYWINKS

Give each child a quarter and a dime. Place dimes around a bowl about a foot away. Take turns flipping the dimes or "winks" into the bowl with the quarter. To flip, hold the quarter between thumb and forefinger and press down on the edge of the dime. The first child to pot his or her wink wins. A young child can play by practicing flipping a dime onto a plate.

THE FEATHER GAME

The players stand close together in a bunch. One of them takes a feather and blows it up into the air. The other players must keep it afloat by their breath. If anyone allows it to sink to the ground he or she must pay a forfeit. Two players can take turns to see who can keep the feather in the air the longest.

Thanksgiving

Start a new family tradition this Thanksgiving by making a book of thanks. Let family members work on their pages during Thanksgiving preparations, and then gather around to read together after dinner. This is a lovely keepsake and a wonderful way to teach children to think about, and be thankful for, all the blessings in our lives.

A BOOK OF THANKS

Handmade book (page 234), *pens, camera and film, glue, scissors*

1. Follow the directions to make your own book. Make sure you have a page for each family member and extra pages for family photographs taken at Thanksgiving (or you can simply hand out pages to family members during Thanksgiving and bind together later).

2. Each person writes his/her name at the top of each page. Ask everyone to answer the following questions (or create a list of your own questions):

   What will you give thanks for this year?

   How are you blessed?

   What is your happiest memory from this year?

   What do you love about Thanksgiving?

   What is your favorite Thanksgiving memory?

   What makes this Thanksgiving special?

3. Help little ones fill their pages with their list of thanks, special Thanksgiving thoughts, and drawings. If possible, have children take Polaroids and glue them into the book. Otherwise, they can add developed pictures later.

Delores's Sunday Special

My stepson, Jay, grew up with his Grandmother Delores's chicken wings and zucchini tomato pie. I couldn't get him to choose one over the other and so share both. You can serve them together.

Honey Glazed Chicken Wings

3 lbs. chicken wings
1 teaspoon salt
1/2 teaspoon pepper
2 tablespoons vegetable oil
1/2 cup honey
1/4 cup soy sauce
1 large can plum tomatoes, crushed
1 clove garlic, minced
2 tablespoons ketchup

1. Preheat oven to 375°F.

2. Put the chicken wings in a shallow pan and sprinkle with salt and pepper.

3. Mix remaining ingredients and pour over wings.

4. Bake 1 hour or until wings are brown.

5. Serve immediately.

Serves four to six.

Zucchini Tomato Pie

2 cups chopped zucchini
1 cup chopped tomato
1/2 cup chopped onion
1/3 cup grated Parmesan cheese
1 1/2 cups milk
3/4 cup Bisquik
3 eggs
1/2 teaspoon salt
1/4 teaspoon pepper

1. Preheat oven to 400°F.

2. Grease a 10-inch pie pan and sprinkle the vegetables into the pan.

3. Beat the remaining ingredients until smooth (about 15 seconds in a blender or 1 minute with a handheld mixer) and then pour over vegetables.

4. Bake approximately 30 minutes, or until an inserted knife comes out clean.

Serves four to six.

Vegetarian Lasagna

This is a great dish to prepare ahead of time before the family arrives. Simply put it into the oven an hour before dinner and then sit down to make the most of your time with your loved ones. Add a simple salad and some bread, and your meal is complete.

1 lb. lasagna noodles
2 tablespoons olive oil
10 ounces ricotta cheese (part skim or
    nonfat ricotta may be substituted)
1 cup pesto sauce
6 cups raw spinach, rinsed and chopped
4 to 5 cups tomato sauce
1 cup tomato paste
3 cups shredded mozzarella cheese
    (part skim or nonfat mozzarella
    may be substituted)

1. Preheat oven to 350°F.

2. In a large stockpot, bring 6 to 8 cups water to a boil. Add pasta and oil; let cook approximately 8 minutes.

3. While pasta cooks, mix ricotta cheese, pesto sauce, and spinach in a large bowl. Set aside.

4. In a large saucepan, heat tomato sauce and tomato paste, stirring until blended. Turn off heat and set aside.

5. Drain pasta and begin assembly. In a 13- x 9-inch baking dish, spread, in order, a thin layer of sauce, pasta, 1/2 ricotta mixture, sauce, pasta, sauce, 1 cup mozzarella, pasta, 1/2 ricotta mixture, sauce, pasta, sauce, 1 cup mozzarella, pasta, and sauce. Finally, top with remaining mozzarella.

6. Cover with aluminum foil and bake approximately 45 minutes. Remove foil and bake another 10 minutes. Let lasagna stand for at least 10 minutes before serving.

Serves eight to ten.

Billy Boy

Oh, __ where have you been, Bil - ly Boy, Bil - ly boy, Oh, __

where have you been, charm-ing Bil - ly? ___ I have

been to seek a wife, She's the joy ___ of my life, She's a

young thing and can - not leave her moth - er. ____

2. Did she ask you to come in, Billy Boy,
      Billy Boy,
   Did she ask you to come in, charming Billy?
   Yes, she asked me to come in, there's a
      dimple in her chin,
   She's a young thing and cannot leave her
      mother.

3. Can she make a cherry pie, Billy Boy...
   She can make a cherry pie, quick as a cat
      can wink an eye...

4. How old is she, Billy Boy...
   Three times six and four times seven,
      twenty-eight and eleven...

233

Bound with Love

Sometimes you can judge a book by its cover. Homemade books bound with love and imagination hint at the importance of what hides inside. Be creative with the book cover, paper, decorative additions, and contents, and you will have a book for any occasion.

HANDMADE BOOK

Paper glue or paste, two 8"x 8" pieces of cardboard, homemade paper (page 254) *or gift wrap, scissors, hole punch, 8"x 2" piece of cardboard, pencil, 8" x 8" sheets of paper, ribbon*

1. Carefully paste handmade paper to the front and back of your cardboard covers. Let dry.
2. Mark four spots for holes along the 8" x 2" piece of cardboard. The first hole will be 1 inch from the top and 1/2 inch in from the edge. Punch the other three holes each 2 inches apart in a straight line below. This will be your hole-punching guide.
3. Use the guide and pencil to mark holes on covers and interior pages. Punch. Stack the covers and pages so the holes align.
4. Cut ribbon into four 6-inches pieces. Thread ribbons through the holes of your book and tie into bows, leaving a little slack so the pages turn easily.

BOOK IDEAS

- Use heavier text stock to make a family photo album.
- Bind together all your secret recipes to make a lasting heirloom.
- Decoupage *(see page 214)* the covers with old Christmas card cutouts to make a family Christmas book.
- Use felt or other fabric to make a soft book for your youngest grandchildren. Sew on felt or fabric shapes.
- Make a "touch and tickle book" using cardboard for the interior. Make cutouts in the cardboard pages and glue interesting textures to the back of each page: feathers, cotton balls, sandpaper, silk.
- Glue foam-core board to the cardboard covers and then cover with a pretty fabric. Bind with narrow strips of the same fabric.
- Bind together a whole book of homemade paper *(see page 254)* to make a beautiful journal.

Little Nanny

Little Nanny Etticoat
In a white petticoat,

And a red nose;

The longer she stands
The shorter she grows.

(a candle)

Etticoat

Thumbelina

nce upon a time there was a young widow who wished to have a little child. She didn't know how she'd manage it, so she went to see a fairy. "Dear fairy, can you tell me where I might find a little child?"

"That's quite easy," replied the fairy. "Here is a rye seed. It is not an ordinary seed like those that grow in the farmers' fields. Take it home and plant it right away."

The widow thanked the fairy and gave her a gold coin. She raced home and planted the seed in a lovely flowerpot. To her amazement, the seed sprouted that very same day, and a beautiful red and gold tulip bud formed. The widow was delighted, and she leaned in to kiss the flower. The petals opened to reveal a tiny girl, no bigger than the widow's thumb. The widow called her Thumbelina.

The widow did her best to make a nice home for Thumbelina. She made her a little bed out of half a walnut shell and placed soft rose-petal blankets inside. A sugar bowl full of water served as

238

Thumbelina

her bathing pool, and one of the tulip petals served as a little boat. Thumbelina would amuse herself in the pool for much of the day. Then, at night, she would crawl between her rose-petal blankets and sing herself to sleep.

One night, a large toad came in through an open window. It jumped right up on the table where Thumbelina lay sleeping in her walnut-shell bed. "What a pretty creature," whispered the toad to herself. "She would make a fine wife for my son." So the toad took Thumbelina, bed and all, and hopped back to the muddy bank of the stream. Her son was even uglier than she was, and when he saw the pretty little girl, all he could say was Croak, croak, croak.

"Shush! Not so loud," said his mother. "You don't want to scare her off. Let's float her shell out to a lily pad in the stream. Meanwhile, we'll prepare a house for you two, here in the mud."

Thumbelina woke early the next morning to find herself stuck in the middle of the stream. She was very frightened and started to cry. Then the toads swam out to get her bed, to place it in the mud house they were building.

"Good morning, dear," said the mother toad. "This is my son, and you shall be his wife. We're building you a mud house, and we'll be back to

Thumbelina

get you when it is ready." Croak, croak, croak, was all her son could say, and they swam away with Thumbelina's bed, leaving her alone on the lily pad.

The fish in the stream heard the mother toad, and now they heard Thumbelina's sobs. They felt sad for the tiny girl, and so decided to help. They gathered under the lily pad and nibbled at the stem: Nibble, nibble, nibble. Finally, the pad broke free of the stem, and Thumbelina's raft floated down the stream.

Happy to be away from the toads, Thumbelina delighted in floating on the water. She watched the sun dance on the tiny waves, as a little breeze caressed her face.

Suddenly, a dragonfly swooped down and caught Thumbelina around the waist. He carried her up into a nearby tree. "You are a beautiful creature," he said. "I should like for you to be my wife." But when the other dragonflies came, they said that she was ugly. They laughed because she had only two legs and no wings. They did not trust her because she looked like the humans, who were the insects' worst enemies. Thumbelina's suitor started to believe what they said, so he carried her down to the ground and left her there.

Thumbelina was glad to be free again, able to enjoy the summer. She wove herself a tiny hammock out of blades of grass.

Thumbelina

She ate berries and nuts that she found. And every morning, she drank the dew that beaded on the leaves and grass.

She soaked up the warmth of summer, and even enjoyed playing in fall's long shadows. But once winter came, Thumbelina grew miserable. When the snowflakes fell, they were like huge ice blankets to a girl of her size. She was chilled to the bone, and knew that she had to find shelter. She traveled to a nearby field, where the remains of the wheat stalks stuck up out of the frozen ground. To her, the cut stalks were like tall trees.

As she walked, she came across a small opening in the ground. It was the entrance to a field mouse's hole. She called down to the mouse, and begged for a piece of grain.

"Come in, poor child," said Mouse. "Sit and eat with me." And when Mouse saw how sweet and lovely Thumbelina was, she invited her to stay for the winter. "You can help me clean the house and tell me stories." So Thumbelina stayed on, and they lived happily together in Mouse's cozy house.

"One of these days soon, we will have a visitor," said Mouse. "My neighbor, Mole, comes about once a week. He is wealthy and wise. He has a big house and wears a velvet coat. If you were to marry him, you would never want for anything. He is blind, and would take comfort in your storytelling."

Thumbelina

Well, Mole did pay a visit, in his black velvet coat. "Please sing for us, Thumbelina," said Mouse. So Thumbelina sang, and Mole fell in love with her lovely voice, but he was too shy to say so.

Mole had recently dug a new tunnel to Mouse's house, and he told Mouse that she and Thumbelina were welcome to use it. "Be warned, however," said Mole. "Someone has buried a dead bird in the tunnel. But don't be afraid of the good-for-nothing, dirty scavenger. He's quite frozen."

Mole's words about the bird upset Thumbelina. "Birds are not good for nothing," she thought to herself. "Their songs are the most beautiful in the world." That night, she could not sleep. She was thinking of the poor frozen bird. She got up and took a bit of hay and raw cotton into the tunnel. She carefully tucked them all around the bird, and said, "Farewell, beautiful swallow. Thank you for your summer songs." She laid her head down on his chest. Then she jumped! She heard a faint thump, thump coming from inside the swallow. She listened again, and it got stronger: THUMP! THUMP! Could it be? Was he still alive?!? Thumbelina was both excited and frightened, for the swallow was a very large creature. She quickly ran back to her bed and grabbed up her blankets to add to his cover.

Thumbelina

The next morning, she went to the tunnel again. The swallow was very weak, but he was alive. "Thank you, thank you, tiny girl," he said. "Soon I will be strong, and I can fly in the sunlight."

"But you can't," cried Thumbelina. "The snow is falling outside, and it is bitter cold. You have missed your chance to fly south, and must wait here until the spring comes. I will take care of you until then." She brought him water in a leaf cup, and little bits of grain that she saved from her dinner. Mole and Mouse never guessed it, but she nursed the swallow all winter long.

When spring arrived, Swallow said, "It is time for me to go. Will you come with me, Thumbelina? I can carry you on my back. We'll stay near the stream until fall, then we will fly south."

"Mouse has been so good to me," she replied. "I'm afraid that my leaving would make her very sad."

"Well, farewell, Thumbelina, and thank you," said the swallow. He darted out of the tunnel and up into the air, singing TWEET! TWEET!

One day, Mouse said, "Today we will start on your wedding dress. You'll marry Mole in the fall, you lucky thing." So Thumbelina and Mouse worked all summer long. Every chance she got, Thumbelina went outside to look for her friend the swallow. But she never saw him.

Thumbelina

Summer came to a close, and the wedding was only a few days off. Thumbelina went to the opening of the mouse's hole, and looked up to the sky. "Good-bye, bright earth," she said. "Goodbye green trees. Goodbye beautiful flowers. Goodbye fresh breezes. Goodbye golden sun!"

Then she heard a gentle song: TWEET! TWEET! She looked around and saw the swallow flying to her. She told him that she was supposed to marry the mole, but was unhappy. "Come with me, instead," said the swallow. "I'm flying south for the winter."

So she climbed on his back, and the swallow flew high into the sky. They traveled over lakes and streams, forests and fields, until they reached the warm country. The sun was as bright as Thumbelina had ever seen it, and it seemed higher, too. She smelled orange blossoms and saw green and red grapes, fat on their vines. Beautiful butterflies of many colors chased alongside of them. Finally, the swallow touched down on a hillside. There were many swallows' nests built into it. "This is my house," he said. Then he flew Thumbelina into the valley and set her down on a lovely pink flower. "This is your house."

Thumbelina was overwhelmed by the beautiful surroundings. Her flower was especially delightful. Suddenly, she saw something move. She looked closer and saw that it was a

Thumbelina

tiny man who also was sitting in the pink flower. He had beautiful brown hair and magical blue eyes. Thumbelina looked around and saw that all the flowers held similar creatures. This one was the king of them all because they all bowed to him.

"Oh, how handsome he is!" whispered Thumbelina.

The swallow had told the king how Thumbelina had saved his life and how sweet and gentle she was. "Would you like to be queen of the flowers?" the little king asked.

"Yes," said Thumbelina. The tiny creatures all greeted the new queen and cheered for the happy couple.

The swallow sang the best songs he knew.

"You shall not be called Thumbelina any more," said the tiny king. "Your new name is Maia."

"Farewell!" called the swallow when he flew back to the north, where he spent his summers. There he made his nest above the window of a storyteller. As he sang — TWEET! TWEET! — The storyteller wrote it all down, and that's how we know the tale of Thumbelina. ✦

247

We can do no great things—
only small things with
great love.

—Mother Teresa

Polly Wolly Doodle

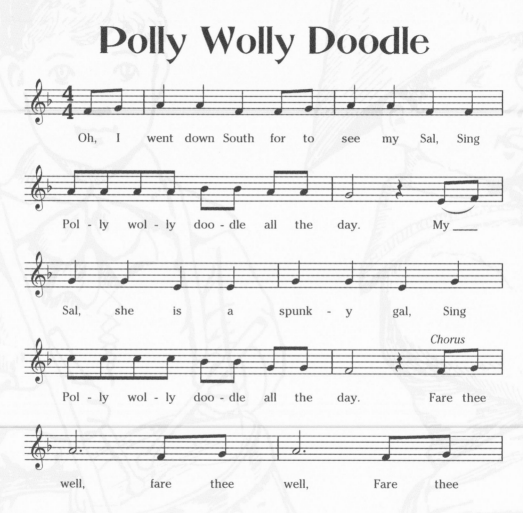

Oh, I went down South for to see my Sal, Sing

Pol - ly wol - ly doo - dle all the day. My ___

Sal, she is a spunk - y gal, Sing

Chorus

Pol - ly wol - ly doo - dle all the day. Fare thee

well, fare thee well, Fare thee

250

Polly Wolly Doodle

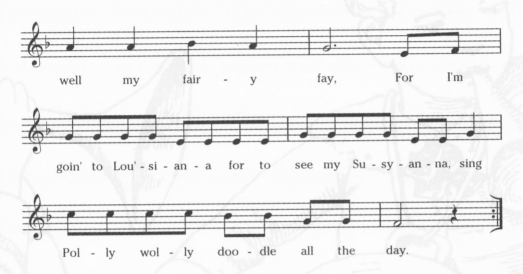

well my fair - y fay, For I'm

goin' to Lou' - si - an - a for to see my Su - sy - an - na, sing

Pol - ly wol - ly doo - dle all the day.

2. Oh, my Sal, she is a maiden fair,
   Sing Polly wolly doodle all the day,
   With curly eyes and laughing hair,
   Sing Polly wolly doodle all the day.

   Chorus

3. Behind the barn, down on my knees…
   I thought I heard a chicken sneeze…

   Chorus

4. He sneezed so hard with the whooping cough…
   He sneezed his head and tail right off…

   Chorus

5. Oh, a grasshopper sittin' on a railroad track…
   A-pickin' his teeth with a carpet tack…

   Chorus

6. Oh, I went to bed but it wasn't any use…
   My feet stuck out like a chicken roost…

   Chorus

This is My Wish for You
by Charles Livingston Snell

This is my wish for you ...

That the spirit of beauty may continually hover about you and fold you close within the tendernesses of her wings.

That each beautiful and gracious thing in life may be unto you as a symbol of good for your soul's delight.

That sun-glories and star-glories, leaf-glories and bark-glories, flower-glories and glories that lurk in the grasses of the field; glories of mountains and oceans of little streams of running waters; glories of song, of poesy, of all the arts may be to you as sweet, abiding influences that will illumine your life and make you glad.

That your soul may be as an alabaster cup, filled to overflowing with the mystical wine of beauty and love.

That happiness may put her arms around you, and wisdom make your soul serene.

This is my wish for you.

252

Homemade Paper

*M*aking beautiful paper is much easier than you think. Try this once and you may find yourself experimenting frequently with different scraps and notions. Use your creations for stationery, cards, picture frames, and book covers (page 234). Let your grandchildren help gather, rip, mix, mash, and roll!

Scrap paper (see Step 1); old window screen; wire cutters; 4 pieces of wood to frame screen; nails and hammer or heavy-duty stapler; blender; water; small flowers, leaves, feathers, or decorative threads; plastic tub large enough to accommodate screen; glue or cornstarch; two large pieces of felt; rolling pin; newspaper; laundry line or twine; clothespins

1. You will need approximately one cup of loosely packed scraps per 8- by 11-inch sheet of paper. Many different colors can be mixed, but it is best to keep the colors light in hue, with little or no printed ink on them, if you plan to use the paper for writing. Choose paper with both long fibers (thicker and harder to rip paper like construction paper) and short fibers.

2. Rip your scrap paper into pieces about 1 inch square. Soak short- and long-fiber paper in separate bowls of water for 15 minutes.

3. Cut your window screen to slightly larger than the paper size you want. Place the screen on top of your four pieces of wood and nail or staple it in place. (Or buy a small, adjustable window screen at a hardware store.)

4. Fill a blender about 3/4 full with clean water. Take a handful of the shorter fiber scraps and put them into the blender. Cover the top and blend on medium-high for a few seconds. The mixture, called pulp, will start to look like runny oatmeal.

5. Add various scraps, short fibers first, one by one, and give a short blast with the blender each time. Don't fill the blender more than 3/4 full.

6. Add decorative items, like threads and flowers, to the mixture, but do not blend.

7. Fill a large tub with clean water. Pour the pulp into the tub and swirl it around. The pulp should be distributed evenly throughout the water before you start dipping.

8. Add a few drops of glue or a tablespoon of cornstarch to the tub and mix it in thoroughly.

9. Hold your screen with the frame on top and dip it in the tub at an angle until it's fully immersed. Move screen back and forth, collecting the pulp on top of it. Lift the screen slowly out of the tub, keeping it flat to catch as much pulp as possible.

10. You should have collected enough pulp on the screen to make one sheet of paper—the pulp should fill the screen evenly to the inner edges of the frame. Allow the water from the pulp to drip off the screen. Hold the frame above the tub until only a few drops of water remain on the screen.

11. Lay a sheet of felt down on a flat tabletop. Turn your frame over on top of the felt. The pulp should drop out easily. If not, you can gently tap the frame on the felt.

12. Lay another felt on top of the pulp. Take a rolling pin and press down on the pile to squeeze out the excess water. Start at one end and roll firmly and evenly across the pile a few times to get as much water out as possible. The rolling action presses the fibers together.

13. Carefully remove the top layer of felt from the pulp.

14. Carefully take up two corners of your paper by rolling them back with your fingers. Hold a corner with each hand and gently peel the sheet off the bottom felt. Use newspaper to absorb any excess moisture from paper.

15. Clip your fresh sheet of paper to the laundry line or twine with clothespins. Leave to dry for a few hours. Avoid damp areas, as mold might grow on the paper.

Here is the Beehive

Here is the beehive.
Where are the bees?

Hidden away
Where nobody sees.

Watch and you'll see them
Come out of the hive—
One, two, three, four, five!

Bzzzz . . .
They're alive!

As I was going to St. Ives
I met a man with seven wives.
Every wife had seven sacks,
Every sack had seven cats,
Every cat had seven kits.
Kits, cats, sacks, and wives,
How many were going to St. Ives?

(one)

Three Little Kittens

by Grace C. Floyd

 nce upon a time there were three little Kittens, who loved to play and frisk about, and run after their own tails and each other's, and anything else that came in their way. One day their mother said, "Now children, I'm going to be very busy, so you can go out to play by yourselves, but be sure you are very good, and don't spoil your neckties nor lose your mittens." Then Mrs. Tabby washed their faces, tied their neckties afresh, put on their mittens, and sent them off. She watched them with pride till they were out of sight, then she bustled back into the kitchen and set to work to make a pie for dinner. "I'll give the children a treat," she thought, "they deserve it for they are the best children in the world and quite the prettiest, and how smart they look in their ties and mittens!" Meanwhile the Kittens were having fine games, and they rolled each other over until they were quiet out of breath and sat down to rest. They were very warm too, so

Three Little Kittens

"The three little Kittens they took off their mittens,
When they had done their play,
But a Jackdaw so sly those six mittens did spy,
And stole them all away."

The Kittens did not notice the Jackdaw, and presently they jumped down off the wall and ran home, quite forgetting all about their mittens. They peeped in at the kitchen door, and there they saw, O, joy! their mother making a pie, a mouse pie too, which they loved more than anything. Then they scampered off again for they knew mother did not like to be disturbed when she was busy, so they had more games until they were called in to dinner. O, how quickly they clambered up on to their little stools, and took up their knives and forks ready to begin; the pie was baked such a lovely brown and it smelt so good! "Good children" said Mrs. Tabby, "now put you ties straight and smooth your mittens,—but where are your mittens?" Then the Kittens looked down at their paws and saw that their mittens were gone, for

"The three little Kittens had lost their mittens,
So they began to cry
'O, Mammy dear, we greatly fear
That we have lost our mittens!'

Three Little Kittens

'Lost your mittens, you naughty Kittens,
Then you shall have no pie'"

said their mother in an angry voice; "Miaou, Miaou, Miaou,"
cried all the poor little Kits, for they were very hungry, "Miaou,
Miaou, Miaou," but Mrs. Tabby was very angry indeed, and she
said, "No, you shall have no pie," and she carried it all lovely,
brown and steaming, away. The three little Kittens cried bitterly
for some time but at last said, "Well, it's no use crying, we must try
to find out mittens." So they wrote in very large letters, on big
sheets of paper, that three pairs of mittens were lost and that any
person who found the same, should have a fine, fat mouse as
reward. Then they pasted these bills up all over the place, and ran
home to hunt for their mittens again. They searched for them
everywhere; they peeped in the saucepan, though, as that had been
on a high shelf all day with the lid on, they could hardly have got
into there, and then they felt in the pockets of their little trousers,
though they could hardly have been there either as they only
wore them on Sundays, and this was Thursday, afterwards they
looked on the wall where they had been sitting and where they
only now remembered that they had hung them but no, they had
gone and were nowhere to be found. But, at last, in the market, in
the old Jackdaw's nest, they found them put out for sale, and Mr.

Three Little Kittens

Jackdaw close by as bold as brass, waiting for customers. Oh, how angry they were! They took old Jack, and they beat him and pulled out his feathers, and though he tried hard to peck, he was only one against three, so it was no use and at last he gave in and the Kittens took their mittens and ran home with them in high glee to their mother calling out "O, Mammy dear, see here, see here, For we have found our mittens!" Mrs. Tabby was highly delighted too, and said, purring proudly and rubbing her paws,

> "Put on your mittens, you good little Kittens
>   And you shall have some pie,
> Yes, you shall have some pie!"

So

> "The three little Kittens, they put on their mittens
>   And soon eat up the pie."

Although it was a very big one, but then they were so hungry and it tasted so good. They felt very happy and comfortable afterwards until they happened to glance at their mittens, and then they saw that they had dropped some gravy on them.

> "O, Mammy dear, we greatly fear
> That we have soiled our mittens,"

Three Little Kittens

whimpered they, for they were honest little Kitties and always told mother directly they had done something naughty, and did not try to hide it.

"Soiled your mittens, you naughty Kittens!" said Mrs. Tabby, and she went and fetched her birch rod, to give them a whipping, so they all three ran off as fast as they could. But they were very sorry that they had made mother so angry, so they put their little heads together, and began to think what they could do to please her. "I know," said the eldest, "Let's wash our mittens." So they crept back to the house, very quietly, so that their mother should not hear, and they lighted the copper fire, and then they got a tub and some hot water, and soap and blue, and they took off their mittens and put them in the tub, and then they rubbed and rubbed, and scrubbed and scrubbed, and boiled and rinsed them until they were quite clean. Mrs. Tabby saw, she did not say anything, but she thought to herself, "I'm sure in all the world there were never such children, they are just as clever as they are pretty." When

"The three little Kittens had washed their mittens
They hung them out to dry,"

The Jackdaw was perched on a bough close by. He looked such a poor miserable old thing, not at all like the sleek Mr.

Three Little Kittens

Jackdaw he was when he stole the three little Kittens' mittens. He said to himself "I could very easily steal those mittens again if I wanted to, but no, never again will I do such a thing, for I'd much rather have my own feathers than other people's mittens." So the little kittens left their mittens hanging on the line to dry, and then ran indoors and said to their mother

> "O, Mammy dear, see here, see here,
> For we have washed our mittens."

Mrs. Tabby gave them each a kiss saying

> "Washed your mittens, you good little Kittens—
> But hark!—I hear a mouse close by,
> To catch him let us try."

So they all scampered after the mouse, and they caught him, and a fine fat mouse he was too. ✦

The Farmer in the Dell

The farm-er in the dell, ____ the farm-er in the dell.

Heigh - ho the der - ry O! The farm - er in the dell. The

farm - er takes a wife, ____ the farm - er takes a wife.

Heigh - ho the der - ry O! The farm - er takes a wife. The

3. The wife takes the child,
The wife takes the child,
Heigh-ho, the derry O!
The wife takes the child.

4. The child takes the nurse...

5. The nurse takes the dog...

6. The dog takes the cat...

7. The cat takes the rat...

8. The rat takes the cheese...

9. The cheese stands alone,
The cheese stands alone,
Heigh-ho, the derry O!
The cheese stands alone.

Homemade Jams

Marty is my marvelous neighbor in San Francisco who went from no grandchildren to five in the space of three years. She is a marvelous cook and believes in starting the day with a delicious breakfast, complete with homemade jams.

RASPBERRY ──────────

2 lbs. fresh raspberries (not too ripe)
4 cups (2 lbs.) white sugar

1. Place the raspberries in a saucepan and crush them slightly with a wooden spoon.
2. Cook over low heat until the fruit bubbles, stirring to keep it from sticking.
3. Add sugar slowly; keep stirring until it dissolves.
4. Increase heat, bringing the jam to a slow boil. Cook without stirring for 10 minutes, until jam sets.
5. Ladle into warmed, sterilized jars and seal while jam is hot.

Makes three cups.

STRAWBERRY ──────────

2 lbs. fresh strawberries (not too ripe)
Juice from one orange
4 cups (2 lbs.) white sugar
1 teaspoon butter

1. Combine strawberries and orange juice in a saucepan over low heat. Bring to a boil and cover; simmer for 15 minutes.
2. Mash gently with a potato masher or a whisk.
3. Add sugar slowly; keep stirring until it dissolves.
4. Increase heat, bringing the jam to a slow boil. Cook without stirring for 10 minutes, until jam sets. Remove from heat and stir in butter.
5. Remove scum. Ladle into warmed, sterilized jars and seal while jam is hot.

Makes three cups.

Embroidery

*E*mbroidery can transform the plainest baby clothes into covetable family heirlooms. *Your grandchildren will love seeing their names stitched onto clothes and on fabric-covered frames and books. Almost anything can be given Grandma's loving touch with embroidery, including towels, pillows, Christmas stockings and even stuffed dolls. When framed, the embroidered words of your grandchild's favorite rhyme or song make a special and thoughtful gift.*

MAKE IT PERSONAL

Disappearing-ink pen, item to embroider, hoop (optional), needle, thread or fine yarn, scissors

1. Carefully trace your grandchild's name in block letters onto your fabric using the disappearing-ink pen. Cotton and linen are good fabric choices if the item is intended for wear.

2. Using a hoop is optional but recommended, as it can help keep your stitches even and prevent puckering in your fabric.

3. Following the instructions below, fill in the outline of each letter of your grandchild's name with the satin stitch. You can stitch each letter in a different color thread or different hues of the same color family to make the design a little more interesting.

4. After you have completed all of the stitches, remove the fabric from the hoop. Lay the embroidered piece face down on a thick terry towel. Carefully press with a warm iron.

5. The finished piece may be framed.

SATIN STITCH

Made at an angle, these parallel stitches fill in the outline of a design that incorporates shape or width. Insert needle from wrong to right side of fabric, coming out at point A. Insert needle at B; pull it back through at C, right next to A. Keep stitches tight and flat to ensure a smooth finish.

B.

A. C.

A

stitch

in

time…

…saves nine.

The Seven Ravens

nce upon a time there was a man who had seven sons. He loved his sons very much, but the man wished for a daughter. At last his wife had another child, and it was a girl! The father wanted to baptize his daughter at once, so he sent his sons down to the river to fetch water.

Well, the boys raced to help their father. In their haste to be the first to the river, they dropped their pitchers into the water. The boys splashed and scrambled after them, but the pitchers floated away. They didn't dare to go home empty-handed.

Meanwhile, their father waited for their return. What was taking so long? Impatiently he hollered, "I wish my naughty sons were all turned into ravens!" No sooner had the words left his mouth when he heard cawing and the sound of wings. Then he saw them: seven black birds flying up into the sky. "What have I done?" he cried.

Sorry as he was to see that his hasty wish had come true,

The Seven Ravens

the man did not know how to undo it. He and his wife tried to comfort themselves for their loss with their dear little daughter. They tried their best to keep the horrible truth from her, but as she grew up, she heard people talk about her seven brothers. The little girl wept. She was very sad to think that it was her birth that had caused her brothers' misfortune. She worried night and day. At last she decided that she would search the world for her brothers and set them free.

On her journey, she took her mother's ring and a loaf of bread. She walked on and on, until she came to the world's end.

Then she came to the sun, but the sun looked much too hot and fiery; so she ran away quickly to the moon, but the moon was cold and chilly; so she ran until she came to the stars, and they were kind to her. The morning star rose up, gave her a little piece of wood, and said, "Use this to unlock the castle that stands on the glass mountain. There you will find your brothers." The little girl took the piece of wood and went on again, until she came to the door of the castle. She took out the little piece of wood, put it in the door, and opened it.

As she went in, a little dwarf came up to her and asked her what she wanted. "I am looking for my seven raven brothers."

278

The Seven Ravens

"They are my masters," said the dwarf, "but they are not at home. I am getting their dinner ready, so please come in and wait." The little dwarf disappeared into the kitchen and returned with seven little plates of food and seven little glasses of water, and set them upon the table. From each little plate, the little girl ate a small piece, and out of each little glass, she drank a small drop; but she let the ring that she had brought with her fall into the last glass.

Suddenly, she heard fluttering and cawing in the air, and the dwarf said, "Here come my masters." When they came in, they went straight for the table and looked for their little plates and glasses.

"Someone has been eating from my little plate," cawed the first brother.

"And someone has been drinking out of my little glass," said the second.

When the seventh came to the bottom of his glass, he found the ring and knew that it was his mother's. All the raven brothers looked at the ring and said, "Has our sister come to find us? Is she here to break the spell?"

When the little girl heard this, she came out from behind the kitchen door. The raven brothers turned back into themselves. They ran to hug their little sister, who had traveled so far and long to find them. Then, with hearts full of joy, they went home. ✦

There was an old woman
tossed in a basket,
Seventeen times as high as the moon;
But where she was going
no mortal could tell,
For under her arm she carried a broom.

"Old woman, old woman, old woman," said I,
"Whither, oh whither, oh whither so high?"
"To sweep the cobwebs from the sky;
And I'll be with you by-and-by."

Old Woman

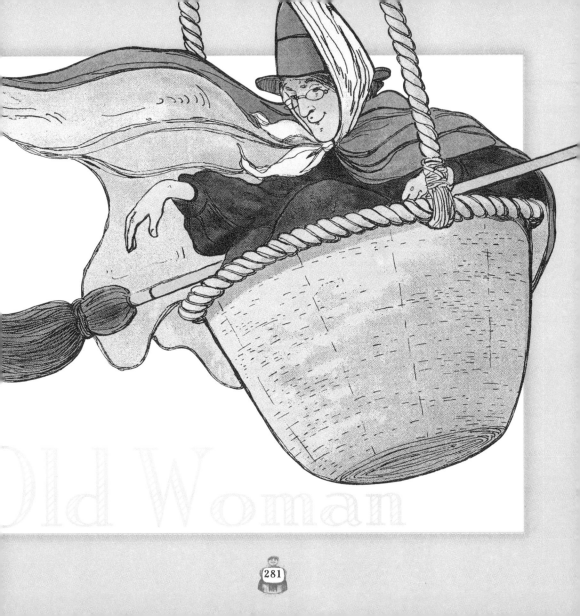

Old Woman

who knows if the moon's

by e. e. cummings

who knows if the moon's
a balloon, coming out of a keen city
in the sky—filled with pretty people?
(and if you and i should

get into it, if they
should take me and take you into their balloon,
why then
we'd go up higher with all the pretty people

than houses and steeples and clouds:
go sailing
away and away sailing into a keen
city which nobody's ever visited, where

always
    it's
        Spring) and everyone's
in love and flowers pick themselves

A Tale of Three Balloons

by Mrs. Albert G. Latham

When kind Granny came to stay with them, she took all the children to the Market, and she bought a lovely red balloon for Rosina, a fine purple one for little Susie, and a bright golden one for Maurice. And after tea Mother said they could all go and play with them on the breezy common where the daisies grew.

"Mine flies best!" cried Rosina. "Look at it! Look at it! I can scarcely hold it in."

"Mine is very naughty," laughed little Susie. "It has bobbed three times against my nose."

Then a shriek came from Maurice:

A Tale of Three Balloons

"Mine's gone! It's gone! Oh, catch it! Catch it!" But his golden treasure went floating up, up, and away.

"I'll help you," cried Rosina. But just then her bonnet ribbons came loose in the wind, twined themselves around the string of her red balloon, and away they sailed together, turning funny somersaults in the air. Rosina grabbed them at last, but the poor red balloon burst in her hands with a horrid pop.

"If it had only been my bonnet that had burst, Mother could have made me a new one," sobbed Rosina, "but she can't make balloons!"

"And oh, look at mine!" wailed Susie. "It has grown as tiny as a plum!"

They went home rather sadly; but at bedtime they were all in the greatest glee, for surely that must be Maurice's lost balloon they could see from the nursery window, shining high up among the golden stars, and brighter than any of them.

And Granny said she would buy them each a new one the very next day. ✖

Balloons

This is the way
We blow our balloon.

Blow!

Blow!

Blow!

This is the way
We break our balloon.

Oh, oh, no!

Windy Days

These activities are all about energy! You can tap into your grandchildren's abundant energy to create and decorate a paper bag kite and a wind chime. Then harness Mother Nature's natural energy—WIND—to make them work!

PAPER BAG KITES

Paper bags, markers, rubber bands, string

1. Help your grandchildren decorate paper bags using markers.

2. Blow air into the bags until they fully inflate like balloons and secure with rubber bands.

3. Attach a long piece of string or ribbon to each bag.

4. Find an open space for each grandchild to run with the paper bag kites. Whose can fly the highest?

WIND CHIMES

Seashells, beads, bells, stones, string or nylon thread, glue, needle, plastic lid

1. Go on a treasure hunt and look for items that will create a lovely sound when they collide, such as seashells, bells, beads, and stones.

2. If the items are thin enough, like seashells, poke a hole through them with a nail. Then pull a piece of string or nylon thread through each hole and tie a knot. For heavier objects such as stones, wrap the string around the object a few times and rub nontoxic liquid glue over the string to hold it in place.

4. Find a colorful plastic lid to serve as the top of the wind chime.

5. Poke holes through the top with a large sewing needle and pull the pieces of string or nylon thread though the holes; tie knots at the ends.

6. Finally, punch two holes in the center of the top and loop a piece of string through the holes, tying a knot on the inside. Hang your wind chime from a nail or the branch of a tree.

Swing, Swing

by William Allingham

Swing, swing,
Sing, sing,
Here! my throne and I am a king!
Swing, swing,
Sing, sing,
Farewell, earth, for I'm on the wing!

Low, high,
Here I fly,
Like a bird through sunny sky;
Free, free,
Over the lea,
Over the mountain, over the sea!

Soon, soon,
Afternoon,
Over the sunset, over the moon;
Far, far,
Over all bar,
Sweeping on from star to star!

No, no,
Low, low,
Sweeping daisies with my toe.
Slow, slow,
To and fro,
Slow—slow—slow—slow.

Snow White and Rose Red

Once upon a time there was a poor widow who had two good and cheerful daughters. They were named Snow White and Rose Red, after the blooms on the two rose trees at the front of their cottage. The girls were the best of friends, and did everything together. At playtime they would run through the meadow, finding flowers for their mother, or they would frolic in the forest, gathering berries and making friends with all the woodland creatures. When it was time for their chores, they worked to keep their mother's cottage neat and tidy. On summer mornings, Rose Red made a wreath of flowers to lay by her mother's bed. On winter evenings, Snow White lit the fire and hung the brightly polished kettle to warm. The sisters would sit by the fire, holding hands, while their mother read to them.

Every night before going to bed, Snow White said, "We must always be together."

Her sister replied, "As long as we live."

Snow White and Rose Red

Their mother would add, "What one has, she must share with the other."

One evening, as they were reading by the fire, someone knocked at the door. Rose Red eagerly jumped up to answer it. But when she unbolted the door, a big, black bear nosed his way into their cottage. Rose Red was startled, and ran. Snow White took cover under her mother's bed. What they didn't know was that this was no ordinary bear. He began to speak. "Please don't be afraid," he said. "I mean you no harm. I am half-frozen, and only wish to get warm."

"Poor bear," said the mother, "lie down by the fire, but be careful not to burn your coat." Then she called, "Snow White, Rose Red, come out. The bear is our guest and our friend."

So the sisters came out, and soon grew comfortable with their new furry friend. They even made a fun routine of his nightly visits: He would come at the same time each night, and they would bring out the broom and sweep the snow from his coat. Then he would stretch out by the fire and let out a great yawn. But the sisters wouldn't let him sleep right away. They tugged his fur, rolled

Snow White and Rose Red

him about, and took turns riding on his back. He would pretend to growl and they would laugh. Sometimes, when they were too rough with the bear, he said, "Please let me live! Are you trying to beat your suitor to death?"

When the snow began to melt away, and the earliest spring flowers were popping through the soil, the bear announced to Snow White that it was time for him to go away for a while. This made her very sad, because she had grown rather fond of the bear. "I must leave you until the leaves fall from the trees," he said. "Then I will return to continue our courtship." Snow White laughed and blushed.

"But where are you going?" she asked.

"I must return to the forest to protect my treasure from the wicked dwarfs," he explained. "When the earth is frozen, they must stay underground in their caves. But in the spring, they break through to the surface and search for treasure."

They said their good-byes, and the bear trotted across the yard and was soon out of sight.

A few days later, their mother sent Snow White and Rose Red to the forest to collect firewood. They walked until they found a great tree that had fallen across a stream. Near the base of the tree, the sisters spotted something moving. As they got closer,

they saw that it was an old dwarf with a long, white beard. The end of his beard was caught in the tree. "Well don't just stand there, you silly girls!" shouted the dwarf. "Help me!"

The girls were shocked to hear him speak to them that way, but they tried in vain to pull him free.

"How did you ever get yourself caught in a tree?" asked Rose Red.

"What's it to you, anyway?" snarled the dwarf.

"Well, I should go find someone to help," she said.

"Why?" asked the dwarf. "You two are already two too many for me! Can't you senseless geese think of something?"

"Don't be so impatient," said Snow White. "I have an idea." She pulled her scissors from her pocket and cut off the end of the dwarf's beard.

"You're more stupid than I thought," said the dwarf. "Cutting a piece from my fine beard will give you bad luck for a year!"

Then the dwarf grabbed a small sack filled with gold, which had been lying in the roots of the tree. He ran off with it slung over his shoulder.

So Snow White and Rose Red gathered some firewood and headed back home. They followed the stream until they saw something moving. As they came nearer, they found the dwarf

Snow White and Rose Red

jumping about like a grasshopper. "Well don't just stand there, you foolish girls!" shouted the dwarf. "Help me! This pesky fish at the end of my line wants to pull me in. I would let him go, but the wind has gotten my beard tangled in my line."

The sisters grabbed hold of the little man and tried in vain to free his beard from the line. Snow White quickly brought out her scissors and cut the beard loose. When the dwarf saw what she had done, he screamed out, "Are you crazy? It wasn't enough that you snipped off the end of my beard. Now you had to cut the best part of it. Your bad luck will never end." Then he picked up a sack of pearls from the tall grass, and without another word, he dragged it away.

The next day, the sisters went to the town to buy needles and thread for their mother. They soon noticed a large bird circling high above their heads. The bird swooped down, and they heard a loud cry. The girls ran over and saw that the eagle held their old acquaintance the dwarf in its talons, and was trying to carry him off.

Snow White and Rose Red

They took hold of him and pulled against the eagle so that it finally let go of its prey. "Couldn't you have been more careful?" cried the dwarf. "You practically pulled my coat apart, you clumsy creatures!" Then he grabbed a sack full of valuable stones and crept under a rock and into his cave. The sisters, who were used to his thanklessness, continued on to town.

On their way home, they surprised the dwarf, who had emptied his bag of gems out onto the road. The sun lit up the brilliant stones, and they glittered and sparkled so beautifully that the girls stood still and stared at them. "Get away from here, you dreadful beings!" the dwarf said in a rage.

Suddenly, a loud growling came from the forest, and a black bear came trotting toward them. The terrified dwarf leaped up and ran, but he could not reach his cave in time. He cried out, "Dear Mister Bear, please spare my life. I will give you all these beautiful jewels. You don't want to eat me, anyway. Take these two tasty girls instead." The bear gave the wicked creature a single strike with his paw, and he did not move again.

Snow White and Rose Red

The sisters started to run, but the bear called to them, "Snow White and Rose Red, don't be afraid." They recognized their friend's voice and turned to see that his bearskin had disappeared. Standing in the bear's place was a handsome man, clothed all in gold. "I am a king's son," he said, "and that wicked dwarf, who stole my treasures, put a curse on me. I have had to live the forest as a wild bear until I was freed by his death. Now he has received his fair reward."

The prince took Snow White to his kingdom, where he married her, and Rose Red married his brother. They shared the great treasure that the dwarf had collected in his cave. Their mother lived peacefully and happily with her children for many years. She brought the two rose trees with her, and they stood before her window. Every year, they produced the most beautiful roses—white and red. ✦

MULBERRY BUSH

The children form into a ring, and holding hands run around singing:

> Here we go round the mulberry bush,
>> the mulberry bush, the mulberry bush;
>
> Here we go round the mulberry bush on a cold
>> and frosty morning.

Then, unloosening hands, they pretend to wash them, singing:

> This is the way we wash our hands,
>> wash our hands, wash our hands;
>
> This is the way we wash our hands on a cold
>> and frosty morning.

They then go around in a ring again, adding verses to wash faces, put on clothes, go to school, and anything they like.

RING AROUND THE ROSEY

At least two players join hands, forming a ring, and walk around singing:

> Ring around the rosey
> A pocket full of posies
> Ashes, ashes,
> We all fall down.

After singing the last line, players collapse to the floor. Then they get up and begin singing all over again.

Oats, Peas, Beans and Barley Grow

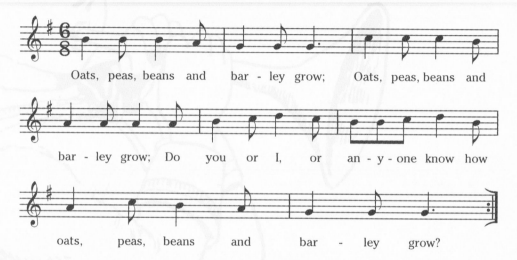

Oats, peas, beans and bar - ley grow; Oats, peas, beans and

bar - ley grow; Do you or I, or an - y - one know how

oats, peas, beans and bar - ley grow?

2. First the farmer sows his seed,
Then he stands and takes his ease;
He stamps his foot and claps his hands,
and turns around to view the land.

3. Waiting for a partner,
Waiting for a partner,
Open the ring and take one in
While we all gaily dance and sing.

·Hilda Austin·

Every Branch of the Family

Discovering genealogy is a terrific family pastime. In these activities you can help your grandchildren, young and old, to understand where they fit in the family tree. It won't take much persuasion to get younger kids to dip their hands in plates of paint, and the naturally inquisitive older kids will jump at the opportunity to interview you and other family members. Work together to collect vital statistics, such as when and where each family member was born, lived, and passed away. Your grandchildren will learn that each family member is like a piece in a puzzle or a leaf on a tree.

FAMILY TREE

notebooks, pencils, large envelopes or plastic boxes (good for keeping the photographs, newspaper clippings, and documents you will collect)

1. The best place to start is with family members your grandchildren know best—themselves! Help the children to record their own full names, birthdays and birthplaces using their birth certificates. Then they can record their immediate family: father, mother, brothers, and sisters.

2. From here you will move backward, one generation at a time. The children can interview cousins, aunts, and uncles, and, of course, you! Encourage them to ask lots of questions and take lots of notes. They should record marriage dates, nicknames, occupations, interesting family stories, and, in the case of dead relatives, record when and where they died. Keep copies of all documentation.

3. Take the children on an excursion to your local courthouse. They have birth, marriage, and death certificates there, and may have the information you need.

4. Your local library may keep old newspapers on microfilm. You can look in the birth and obituaries sections. The obituaries will usually list the surviving family members. Ask if they have census records for the city too.

5. If the person you are looking for was born after 1930 you can contact the

Social Security office and request the records of that person. Their application forms will contain the date of birth, date of death, and who their parents were.

6. When you have finished compiling all of your historical data you can create a chart to illustrate your tree.

7. A family tree is a unique and special gift to a new grandchild. Add the name and date of birth of your newest grandchild—the newest blossom on your family tree. Frame and hang in your little darling's nursery.

HANDPRINT FAMILY TREE

Paint (in assorted colors), paintbrush, paper plates, white cotton fabric (an old sheet works well), permanent marker, fabric glue, 12-inch-long strong stick or wooden dowel, a long piece of string or ribbon

1. Paint a tree trunk with bare branches on the fabric.

2. Ask each of your grandchildren to pick out their favorite color from your selection of paints and spread a little of each color on paper plates.

3. Working from biggest to littlest hands, have each child dip his/her hands in their chosen paint and print them on the branches. Ask other family members—parents, aunts, uncles etc.—to get their "hands dirty" also to make your tree more complete.

4. Use permanent markers to write names next to handprints.

5. Children can paint birds, sky, sun, grass, and flowers etc. to complete the scene. Let dry.

6. Fold over a few inches at the top of the fabric and glue the edge to the back to form a sleeve for your stick or dowel. When the glue is dry, slide the stick or dowel through the sleeve.

7. Tie your ribbon or string to each end of the stick to make a hanger for your masterpiece. Ask your grandchildren to help you find the perfect place to display your family banner.

Nothing happens
unless first a dream.

—Carl Sandburg

The Road Not Taken

by Robert Frost

Two roads diverged in a yellow wood,
And sorry I could not travel both
And be one traveler, long I stood
And looked down one as far as I could
To where it bent in the undergrowth;

Then took the other, as just as fair,
And having perhaps the better claim,
Because it was grassy and wanted wear;
Though as for that, the passing there
Had worn them really about the same,

And both that morning equally lay
In leaves no step had trodden black.
Oh, I kept the first for another day!
Yet knowing how way leads on to way,
I doubted if I should ever come back.

I shall be telling this with a sigh
Somewhere ages and ages hence:
Two roads diverged in a wood, and I—
I took the one less traveled by,
And that has made all the difference.

Grandmother's Path

Grandmother's house stood next door to Bobby's. Across the lawn which stretched between the two houses there was a little path of red bricks. It led from the side door of Grandmother's house to the side door of Bobby's house. Bobby called it Grandmother's path, because she used it when she came to see Bobby and his little sister, Baby Jane. Every morning Bobby stood at the side window and watched for their daily visitor. And when she opened her door he would call out, "Grandmother's coming, Mother! She'll tell us another story."

And Baby Jane in the nursery would laugh and coo as if she wanted to say, "Grandmother's coming, Mother."

Grandmother's Path

One winter day a deep snow lay all over the ground. Early in the morning you couldn't see Grandmother's path at all; but before Father left for the office he took his big snow shovel and cleared all the snow away from the bricks.

Later in the morning Bobby stood at the window waiting for Grandmother.

"Mother," he said, "it's been snowing again. Look at Grandmother's path."

Mother stepped to the window and said, "So it has. And Grandmother's path is covered again. I hope some boy who can use a snow shovel will come this way."

"I can use one, Mother," said Bobby. "I watched Father use his. Let me clear Grandmother's path!"

"You shall begin it, dear," laughed Mother. "But the shovel is a pretty big shovel for such a little man to use. We'll see how much of the path you can clear."

Grandmother's Path

Then Mother helped Bobby to put on his blue woolen suit, his blue woolen leggings, and his pointed woolen cap with the tassel. She put Father's big snow shovel into his hands and he began to push it through the snow along Grandmother's path.

It was hard work, and after Bobby had cleared a little way he stopped to rest, looking toward Grandmother's door. He wondered if he could ever reach it.

Just then the baker's boy came with bread and rolls. He looked a little surprised when he saw Bobby and the big snow shovel. But he nodded cheerfully and said,

"Snow Shovel and you, my little man,
Are working hard today.
Little by little, step by step,
You'll clear the snow away."

Grandmother's Path

"It's Father's snow shovel," said Bobby. "I'm making a path for Grandmother."

Then he worked away as hard as he could. And when half of the path was cleared he stopped again to rest, looking toward Grandmother's door.

And while he was resting, the milkman came. He, too, looked surprised when he saw Bobby and the big snow shovel. But he nodded cheerfully and said,

> "Snow shovel and you, my little man,
> Are working hard today.
> Little by little, step by step,
> You'll clear the snow away."

Grandmother's Path

And Bobby said, "It's Father's snow shovel. I'm making a path for Grandmother."

He worked away again until he had nearly reached Grandmother's door. He stopped to rest once more, feeling sure now that he could finish the path.

In a few moments the grocer's boy came hurrying along with a basket full of groceries which he was taking to Grandmother's house.

He called out, "Hurrah for Bobby and his big snow shovel!"

"It's Father's snow shovel," answered Bobby. "I cleared a path for Grandmother."

And the grocer's boy laughed and said cheerfully,

Grandmother's Path

"Snow shovel and you, my little man,
Had a hard task today.
But little by little, step by step,
You've cleared the snow away."

For Bobby was now at Grandmother's door. Out she stepped, saying, "What a nice clean path my little man has made for me to-day." She took Bobby's hand and they both walked along the clean path to see Baby Jane.

Listen To The Mustn'ts

Listen to the MUSTN'TS, child,
Listen to the DON'TS
Listen to the SHOULDN'TS
The IMPOSSIBLES, the WON'TS
Listen to the NEVER HAVES
Then listen close to me—
Anything can happen, child,
ANYTHING can be.

Hug O' War

I will not play at tug o' war.
I'd rather play at hug o' war,
Where everyone hugs
Instead of tugs,
Where everyone giggles
And rolls on the rug,
Where everyone kisses,
And everyone grins,
And everyone cuddles,
And everyone wins.

by Shel Silverstein

Follow-the-Leader

An active and daring child should be chosen as leader. The others follow him or her, one behind the other, as closely as they can, doing as the leader does and going where the leader goes. The leader can choose to hop, skip, and jump; or crawl under and climb over obstacles. If anyone fails to accomplish any one feat, he or she leaves the line. The final person left in the line becomes the next leader.

SIMON SAYS

One child is "Simon." The other children spread out near Simon and wait for his directions. Simon will give the group commands, like "touch toes," "rub belly," "hop on one foot," etc. If Simon precedes each command with the phrase "Simon says" the group has to follow his command. If his directions are not preceded with "Simon says," anyone who follows the command is out of the game. The last person in the game wins and is Simon in the next round. An adult can play this game with one child to test his or her concentration and focus.

TUG-OF-WAR

Find a strong, long rope and tie a piece of string at its center. Lay the rope down and and draw a corresponding line on the ground to show where the center is. The children divide into two groups and line up behind one another, holding on to opposite ends of the rope. On the signal "ready, set, go," both teams pull the rope as hard as they can. The children tug and tug until one team wins by forcing the other team to step over the line marked on the ground.

Goosey, Goosey, Gander

Goosey, goosey, gander,

    Whither dost thou wander?

Upstairs and downstairs

    And in my lady's chamber.

323

Christmas Wreaths

A wreath is an attractive, easy-to-make decoration for the holiday season. The hand-print wreath is easy for younger children to make and will bring a smile each year at holiday time remembering just how little those hands were! The holiday wreath is a fun project for older children. Use strongly scented greens like juniper and pine.

HANDPRINT WREATH

Green construction paper, pencil, scissors, paper glue or paste, red construction paper

1. Let your grandchildren trace their hands on green construction paper. Cut out.

2. Glue one handprint to another, over-lapping slightly to form a circle.

3. Glue on small circles cut out of red paper for holly berries. Add a red paper bow to finish.

HOLIDAY WREATH

Wreath frame (15-inch), roll of florist wire, evergreen branches, pruning shears, wire cutter, ribbon bow, pine cones, holly

1. Buy your wreath frame from a craft store or make one using a wire coat hanger.

2. Attach the end of your florist wire to the frame.

3. Cut the evergreen branches into 4- to 6-inch sections with the shears. Place a small bundle of greens on the frame and fasten tightly with two or three turns of the wire.

4. Place a second bundle of greens on the frame, covering the base of the first group, and secure with wire. Continue with remaining greens. Tuck the base of the final bundle of greens beneath the foliage of the first bundle. Trim off excess wire.

5. Fasten bow, cones, and holly with wire to decorate.

The Little Match Girl

Once upon a time, it was New Year's Eve, and it was very dark and cold. Snowflakes fell thick and fast. A poor little girl wandered through the empty streets without a hat or shoes. In her hands she carried bundles of matches. All day long she had tried to sell her matches, but no one had bought a single one—she had not earned a single penny. Trembling with cold and hunger, she continued to walk through the icy streets. Beautiful lights twinkled in all the windows, and the wonderful smell of roast goose filled the air.

Finally, the little girl had grown too cold and tired to go on. She crouched down in a corner between two houses and tucked her feet under her. She tried to use her shawl as a shield against the wind, but it was no use—the cold went right through her. She didn't dare go home. Her father would be angry that she hadn't made a single sale. It wouldn't be much warmer there anyway. The wind whipped through her attic home almost as violently as outside.

The Little Match Girl

The little girl's fingers were nearly frozen. If only she could light a match! But what would her father say at such waste! Shyly, she took out a match and lit it. What a nice warm flame! The little girl cupped her hand over it, and as she did so, a big brightly burning stove magically appeared. She held out her hands to the heat, but just then, the match went out and the vision faded.

After hesitating for a long time, she struck another match on the wall, and this time, the glimmer turned the wall into a great sheet of crystal. Beyond the crystal sheet stood a fine table set with a feast. Holding out her arms toward the plates, it seemed to the little girl that she passed through the glass, but then the match went out and the magic faded.

She lit a third match, and an even more wonderful thing happened. There stood a Christmas tree hung with hundreds of candles. "Oh, how lovely!" exclaimed the little girl. Then the match flickered out. But the Christmas candles rose higher and higher, until they looked to her like stars in the sky. One of the lights fell, leaving a trail behind it.

"Someone is dying," murmured the little girl as she

The Little Match Girl

remembered her beloved grandmother, who used to say, "Each time a star falls, a soul flies up to God."

The little girl lit another match, and there before her appeared her departed grandmother, gentle and loving as ever. "Grandma, stay with me!" she pleaded, as she lit one match after another, so that her grandmother could not disappear, like all the other visions. But her grandmother did not vanish, and continued to smile down at her. Then she opened her arms and the little girl hugged her, crying: "Grandma, take me away with you!"

The two flew away together, overwhelmed with happiness. They flew far above the earth, higher and higher, until they were in the place where neither cold nor hunger nor pain is ever known.

A cold day dawned, and some passersby discovered the lifeless body of a little girl crouched in a corner. Her cheeks were pale and her hands were blue, but a smile was on her face. "Poor little thing!" the people exclaimed, seeing the burned matches. "She was trying to keep warm!" But none of them could know what beautiful things she had seen, or the joy she had felt entering into the New Year with her grandmother. ✦

Pecan Pie

How does one make pecan pies? Toasted, roasted, perhaps stir-fried? No, they actually come from Granny's oven—made with flour, patience, and lots of lovin'.

PASTRY

12 tablespoons (1 1/2 sticks) cold
    unsalted butter, cut into little pieces
3 cups all-purpose flour
3 tablespoons sugar
2 egg yolks, lightly beaten
About 1/4 cup ice water

FILLING

5 whole eggs
1 egg yolk
1 cup packed light brown sugar
2 tablespoons melted butter
2 teaspoons vanilla extract
2 to 3 tablespoons bourbon
3 cups pecan pieces, lightly toasted

1. In a mixing bowl, cut butter into the flour until it reaches the consistency of fine meal.

2. Sprinkle on the sugar and add lightly beaten egg yolks and ice water. Lightly blend together. Shape the dough firmly into a ball, wrap in waxed paper, and chill for at least 20 minutes.

3. Preheat oven to 350°F.

4. In a bowl, mix together all the filling ingredients except the pecans and blend well.

5. Roll out pastry on a lightly floured surface and fit it into a 9" pie pan. Place a layer of pecan pieces on the pastry. Pour filling mixture over the nuts. Bake for 1 hour, or until golden brown.

6. Cool to room temperature before serving.

Makes one 9-inch pie.

Girls

Girls and boys come out to play,
The moon doth shine as bright as day,
Leave your supper and leave your sleep,
And come with your playfellows into the street.

Come with a whoop, come with a call,
Come with a good will, or come not at all.

Up the ladder and down the wall,
A halfpenny bun will serve us all.
You find milk and I'll find flour.
And we'll have pudding in half an hour.

Family Quilt

A handmade quilt can become a most treasured and beloved family heirloom. Sew simple shapes like stars, moons, and letters to the quilt squares to make a small crib quilt for your expected grandchild. Present your growing grandchild with a quilt made from favorite outgrown baby clothes, blankets, or crib bedding when they move to their first "grown-up" bed. Let older grandchildren each contribute special squares to be sewn together into a beautiful quilt that tells the story of your family.

Scissors, an iron, patterned and plain fabric pieces cut into $4\frac{1}{2}$" x $4\frac{1}{2}$" squares, straight pins, needle and thread, 66" x 96" twin flat sheet, thin quilt batting or flannel fabric, darning needle, wool yarn

1. Iron squares and arrange them on the floor in 24 rows of 18 squares, creating a pleasing pattern.
2. To sew the first row, place the second square on top of the first, front sides facing each other. Pin along one side of the square and sew a $\frac{1}{4}$-inch seam down this side. Remove pins.
3. Pin and sew the third square to the second square in the same manner. Continue until all eighteen squares.
4. With front sides facing each other, pin and sew the first and second rows together along one edge. Repeat until all eighteen rows are sewn together. Iron all seams flat.
5. Place your batting or flannel material on the backside of the quilt top and stitch it loosely to hold it together (these stitches may be removed later).
6. Smooth a bedsheet out on the floor and center your quilt on top of the sheet, front side down, batting facing up. Pin together.
7. Sew a $\frac{1}{4}$-inch seam around your quilt, leaving a 6-inch opening in the middle of one side. Remove pins.
8. Turn your quilt right side out through the opening. Stitch opening closed.
9. Iron the quilt and lay it out on the floor. Hold the thickness of the quilt together using pins. Push the darning needle threaded with wool yarn through the middle of a quilt square, leaving about 5 inches of yarn on top. Push the needle back through the quilt from back to front and cut the yarn, leaving another 5 inches. Tie the pieces of yarn together in a square knot. Trim ends. Repeat in the middle of each square. Remove pins.

Good ... Children

by Robert Louis Stevenson

Children, you are very little,
And your bones are very brittle;
If you would grow great and stately,
You must try to walk sedately.

You must still be bright and quiet,
And content with simple diet;
And remain, through all bewild'ring,
Innocent and honest children.

Happy hearts and happy faces,
Happy play in grassy places—
That was how, in ancient ages,
Children grew to kings and sages.

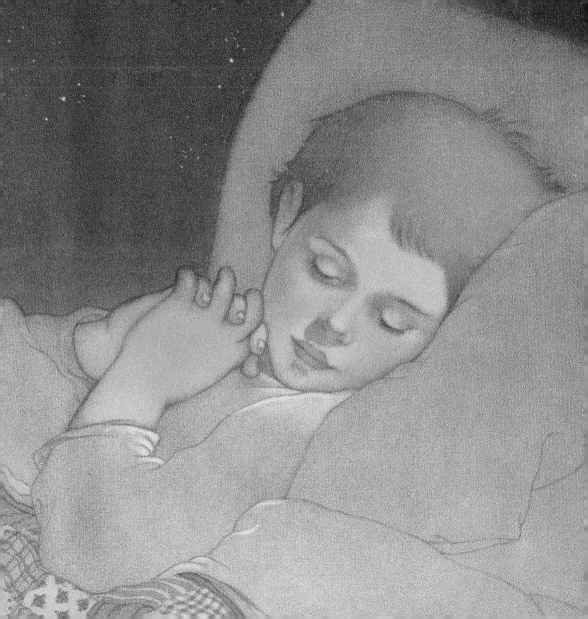

Ned's Visit to His Grandmother

by Marion Walton

"Mother, I'd like to take Grandmother something in my little red cart," said Ned. "What shall I take her?"

"Here are some cookies I have just made for her tea. Take some of them," said his mother.

"That will be the very thing," said the little boy. "And I'll take her an apple, too."

Mother put a piece of white paper around the cookies and tied it with a pink string. And Ned put a piece of white paper around the apple and tied it with pink string. Then he put both into his little red cart and started for Grandmother's house.

Ned's Visit to His Grandmother

He soon came to a barn. Little White Hen was standing at the door. As soon as she saw Ned and his little cart coming down the road she stepped out to meet him. Right up to the little red cart she went and sniff sniff! She smelled the cookies and apple.

"Good morning, Little White Hen," said Ned.

"Cluck, cluck!" said Little White Hen. That was her way of saying, "I want some cookies."

"No, no, Little White Hen," said Ned. "You may not have any of the cookies or the apple. I am taking them to Grandmother. Come with me to her house. Perhaps Grandmother will let you have some of the crumbs."

So Little White Hen followed behind Ned's cart.

They had not gone far before they came to a house by the roadside. Lying on the doorstep was Little Gray Kitten. As Ned and his little red cart drew near she opened her sleepy eyes.

When she saw them, she jumped up from the doorstep and ran out to meet them. Soon she smelled the cookies and the apple in the cart. Right up to it she went and began to sniff.

"Good morning, Little Gray Kitten," said Ned.

"Mew, mew, mew," said Little Gray Kitten. That was her way of saying, "I want some cookies."

"No, no, Little Gray Kitten," said Ned. "You may not have any of the cookies or the apple. I am taking them to Grandmother. Come with us to her house. Perhaps Grandmother will let you have some of the crumbs."

So Little Gray Kitten followed Ned, his little red cart, and Little White Hen.

It wasn't long before they came to a field by the roadside. In the field was a little fat pig. The pig saw Ned and his cart. So he slipped under the fence and ran out to meet them. Right up to the

Ned's Visit to His Grandmother

little red cart went Little Pig. When he smelled the cookies and the apple he put his snout right into the little red cart.

"Good morning, Little Pig," said Ned.

Little Pig said, "Wee, wee!" That was his way of saying, "I want some cookies."

"Oh, no, Little Pig," said Ned. "You may not have any of the cookies or the apple. I am taking them to Grandmother. Come with

us. Perhaps Grandmother will let you have some of the crumbs."

So Little Pig went with Ned, his little red cart, Little White Hen, and Little Gray Kitten.

Soon Ned saw Grandmother's house. But just then a little brown bird in a tree saw Ned, his little red cart, Little White Hen, Little Gray Kitten, and Little Pig. Down he flew from the tree and peeped right into the little red cart. He soon found out that there was something good to eat in it.

"Good morning, Little Bird," said Ned.

"Peep, peep," said Little Bird. That was his way of saying, "I want some cookies."

"Oh, no, Little Bird," said Ned. "You may not have any of the cookies or the apple. I am taking them to Grandmother. Come with us. Perhaps she will let you have some of the crumbs."

So Little Bird went along with Ned, his little red cart,

Ned's Visit to His Grandmother

Little White Hen, Little Gray Kitten, and Little Pig.

Grandmother was looking out of the window. All at once she saw something queer coming down the road.

"What do I see?" she said. She looked and looked. She took off her glasses and rubbed them, put them on, and looked again.

Oh, it's little Ned. But who are following him?"

She hastened to the door. There she saw coming through the gate, Ned, and behind him came his little red cart, and behind the little red cart came Little White Hen, and behind Little White Hen came Little Gray Kitten, and behind Little Gray Kitten came Little Pig, and behind Little Pig came Little Bird.

"Well, well, well," said Grandmother. She was so surprised that that was all she could say.

Then Ned told Grandmother why Little White Hen and Little Gray Kitten and Little Pig and Little Bird had come

Ned's Visit to His Grandmother

along with him. And Grandmother sat right down on the
doorstep and ate the cookies and the apple. She left big crumbs,
too—some for Little White Hen, some for Little Gray Kitten,
some for Little Pig, and some for Little Bird.

While they were eating the crumbs, she and Ned went into
the house. She gave him a bowl of cornmeal for Little White
Hen, a saucer of milk for Little Gray Kitten, a pan of milk for
Little Pig, and a handful of bread crumbs for Little Bird. And
what do you think she gave Ned for himself? A saucer of
strawberries and cream. So they all had a picnic out in
Grandmother's backyard.

When it was time to go home, Ned kissed Grandmother and
said, "We must go now. Thank you for the good dinner."

And Grandmother kissed Ned and said, "Good-by, Ned.
I've had a happy time, too."

Ned's Visit to His Grandmother

The little boy opened the gate and went out with his little red cart. Behind him came Little White Hen, behind Little White Hen came Little Gray Kitten, behind Little Gray Kitten came Little Pig, and behind Little Pig came Little Bird.

As they were going through the gate Little White Hen said, "Cluck, cluck!" That was her way of saying, "Thank you."

Little Gray Kitten said, "Mew, mew." That was her way of saying, "Thank you."

Little Pig gave two big grunts. That was his way of saying, "Thank you."

And Little Bird said, "Peep, peep." That was his way of saying, "Thank you."

And Grandmother called out, "You are quite welcome, my friends."

Sleep, Baby, Sleep

Sleep, baby, sleep,
Our cottage vale is deep:
The little lamb is on the green,
With woolly fleece so soft and clean—
  Sleep, baby, sleep.

Sleep, baby, sleep,
Down where the woodbines creep;
Be always like the lamb so mild,
A kind, and sweet, and gentle child.
  Sleep, baby, sleep.

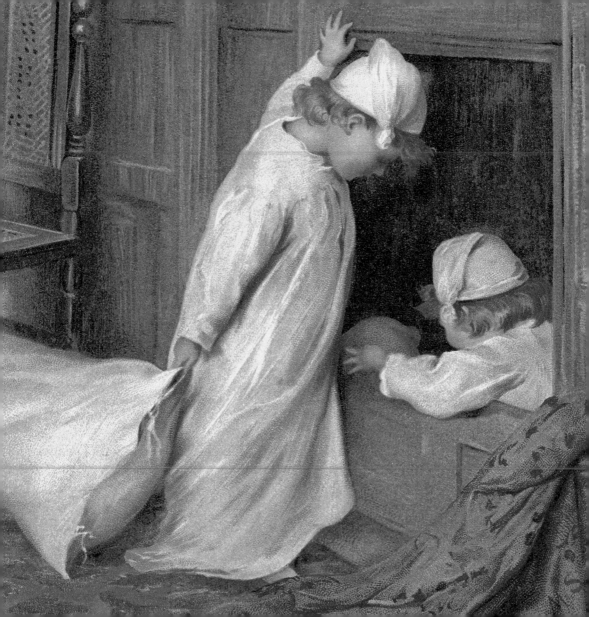

Granny's Gone to Sleep

by Matthias Barr

Granny's gone to sleep:
Softly, little boys;
Read your pretty books,
Don't make a noise,
Pussy's on the stool,
Quiet as a mouse;
Not a whisper runs
Through the whole house.
Hush! silence keep; Granny's gone to sleep.

Enjoy yourself. These are the
"good old days" you're going
to miss in the years ahead.

—Anonymous

ACKNOWLEDGMENTS

"The Frog" Reprinted by permission of PFD on behalf of: *The Estate of Hilaire Belloc* ©: as printed in the original volume.

"who knows if the moon's". Copyright 1923, 1925, 1951, 1953, © 1991 by the Trustees for the E.E. Cummings Trust. Copyright © 1976 by George James Firmage, from COMPLETE POEMS: 1904-1962 by E.E. Cummings, edited by George J. Firmage. Used by permission of Liveright Publishing Corporation.

"The Road not Taken" from THE POETRY OF ROBERT FROST edited by Edward Connery Lathem, © 1969 by Henry Holt and Co. Reprinted by permission of Henry Holt & Co., LLC.

"I'd Love to Be a Fairy's Child" by Robert Graves from FAIRIES& FUSILIERS. Reprinted by permission of Carcanet Press Limited.

"The Little Turtle" Reprinted by permission of Scribner, a Division of Simon & Schuster, Inc., from THE COLLECTED POEMS OF VACHAL LINDSAY, REVISED EDITION by Vachel Lindsay. (New York: Macmillan, 1925)

"Little Red Caboose" by Deke Moffitt Reprinted by permission of Carl Fischer Music

"Tale of Custard the Dragon" Copyright © 1936 by Ogden Nash, renewed Reprinted by permission of Curtis Brown, Ltd.

"Baby Beluga" Words by Raffi, D. Pike. Music by Raffi. © 1980 Homeland Publishing (SOCAN). A division of Troubadour records Ltd. All rights reserved. Used by permission.

"HUG O' WAR" and "LISTEN TO THE MUSTN'TS" by Shel Silverstein. Copyright © 1974 by Evil Eye Music, Inc.

JELL-O® is a registered trademark of Kraft Foods, Inc.

ILLUSTRATIONS

Cover, pg. 173: Jessie Wilcox Smith; pg. 1, 37, 40-41, 94, 133, 166-167, 224, 301, 320: Kate Greenaway; pg. 17, 61, 75, 189,196, 290, 325: Margaret Evans Price; pg. 22: Flora C. Twort; pg. 25: Fern Bisel Peat; pg. 43: A. Macgregor; pg. 66: E. Clart; pg. 84, 87: N. Buchanan; pg. 91, 202-203: Eul Alie; pg. 100: J.H. Hartley; pg. 113, 147, 150, 297: Frances Brundage; pg. 115: Frank Hart; pg. 119: Rosa C. Petherick; pg. 123: Maud Humphrey; pg. 129: Helena Maguire; pg. 143: Lenski; pg. 158: John Winsch; pg. 198-199: Blanche Fisher Wright; pg. 221: Torrey; pg. 232: T.J.R.; pg. 274-275: N. Westrup; pg. 277: Anne Anderson; pg. 286: E. Dorothy Rees; pg. 289, 303: Hilda Austin; pg. 319: Shel Silverstein; pg. 328: E.S. Hardy; pg. 334: Mary Sherwood & Wright Jones; pg. 341: Ellen H. Clapsaddle; pg. 347: Ruth Steed